# SON & SHIELD

SIGNS OF LIFE SERIES
BOOK 5

CRESTON MAPES

STAND-ALONE THRILLERS
*I Am In Here*
*Nobody*


SIGNS OF LIFE SERIES
*Signs of Life*
*Let My Daughter Go*
*I Pick You*
*Charm Artist*
*Son & Shield*
*Secrets in Shadows*


THE CRITTENDON FILES
*Fear Has a Name*
*Poison Town*
*Sky Zone*


ROCK STAR CHRONICLES
*Dark Star: Confessions of a Rock Idol*
*Full Tilt*

*Thanks to the team at the Portland Police Bureau for answering my many questions about everything from training and wages to equipment, weapons, personnel, and procedures.*

*Gratitude to the Sedona Police Department (carried over from my last book) for insights about police training, shifts, schedules, pay, reviews, and life on the job.*

*Grateful for friend-author-cop Mark Mynheir for always being available to answer my questions about police procedures.*

*Special thanks to my early reader team for their time and insights: Patty Mapes (wink, wink), Vicki Burke, Gail Mundy, Diane Moody, Lynelle Murrell, Rachel Savage, and Ginger Aster.*

# 1

"Lastly . . . listen up, please. Before I turn you loose, I'm sure you've all noticed we have a new man in uniform with us today." Towering, broad-shouldered Portland Police Sergeant Dolby Tidwell neared the end of his early morning briefing to the large group of uniformed officers and plain clothes detectives. Before Tidwell could say another word, officers clapped and whistled. Tidwell raised his voice. "Everybody, please give Officer Brandon Deetz a warm welcome to the Portland Police Bureau."

The cheers and laughter got louder, and Brandon grinned shyly, blushed, and gave a small nod and wave.

Sitting across the full room from his son, Investigator Wayne Deetz clapped and smiled proudly, a bit embarrassed himself by the eyes that fell to him. Deetz's colleagues normally wouldn't welcome a new officer with such zeal—especially at seven in the morning—but they did so, knowing Deetz would be ending his thirty-five-year career in eight months, and his son Brandon would be following in his footsteps.

"Brandon not only completed his sixteen-week State Basic Academy, but he earned enough college credits to graduate with his bachelor's degree later this month." Tidwell nodded kudos to Brandon and stroked a large hand over his bald head, which gleamed like a newly waxed car beneath the staging area's fluorescent lights. "Brandon also earned a marksman medal and I've been

I

told he's one of the finest shots we've had come through the Academy in a long time. Guess Wayne got him started early."

More laughter broke out as Deetz recalled his shock when he and Joanie had returned home in December from their vacation in Sedona, Arizona, and Brandon told them he had joined the force and was entering Basic Academy at the beginning of the new year. They'd been flabbergasted and had begun to protest, because Brandon only had one semester remaining before he was due to graduate from college. But he'd assured them he would receive more than enough credits during his police training to graduate on time in May.

Joanie still wasn't pleased about his decision to become a cop—for a million reasons.

Glancing across the room at the twenty-three-year-old man Brandon had become, Deetz was dumbstruck at how fast the years had flown past. Brandon had been the one of their three children who, as a baby, constantly craned his neck to see where they were going next. He was always up for an adventure, rarely cried, and constantly exhibited a positive outlook.

Now, here they were two decades later—May 2, 2022—and Brandon was decked out in his Portland Police blues, ready to hit the streets with a standard-issued 9mm Glock 17 strapped to his side. The past two years he'd developed a love for guns and almost an obsession with target practice. Deetz had to admit, he was proud his son had become an even better marksman than him. And Brandon's starting pay—thanks to Portland City Council's vote on a Collective Bargaining Agreement—was a whopping sixty-seven thousand dollars.

*Not too shabby for twenty-three years old.*

Deetz really couldn't imagine Brandon in any kind of sedentary desk job, although he'd hoped he might go to work for Nike, with whom he'd recently completed a successful internship.

Tidwell—whose eyes were shadowed by dark, swollen half-circles—waved a hand toward Brandon's dad. "You may've also noticed that our beloved and decorated veteran Detective Wayne Deetz is dressed out in his traditional police blues today. Been a long time since we've seen you in those." The room erupted with ovations and laughter. "Brandon will have the privilege of riding with his dad during his field training, and he'll attend Advanced Academy whenever we have the next class. With our budget the way it is, I'm not sure when that will be."

Tidwell was a huge man, probably two-hundred-and-sixty pounds. He moved slowly as he spoke and seemed sad, as if burdened by some unseen weight. Deetz wondered if he might be having troubles in his private life. Or perhaps he was just down because of the political conflicts within the city government of late. Tidwell made eye contact with Brandon and said, "I'm sure you know you couldn't be learning from a finer officer. Your dad is definitely one of the good ones." Brandon nodded, his cheeks pink. Tidwell turned to Deetz and said, "Show him how it's done, Wayne. We need more like you."

A young female officer whom Deetz didn't recognize raised a hand and asked if any special precautions were being put in place as the city approached the four-year anniversary of the May 7th mass shooting on Pioneer Square downtown, coming up in five days. As Tidwell began to address the question, a bittersweet and foreboding feeling came over Deetz.

Policing today had become an entirely different beast than it was when Deetz started his career in the mid-eighties. Crime and riots were now rampant in Portland. The evils of man had arisen to blatant extremes on the streets. Hate, discord, and rebellion were almost palpable. Gang attacks and retaliatory shootings were skyrocketing, with multiple shootings each week and more bullets flying than ever before—often hitting innocent bystanders like city workers and delivery drivers. Homicides in Portland were up two thousand percent from the previous year. And to make matters worse, cops were being watched, recorded, judged, and scrutinized for every move they made.

Being back in uniform, Deetz was slightly nervous about all the eyes—and cameras—that would be upon him. Everyone had a phone with a camera these days, not to mention all the recording devices throughout the city and hooked up to homes. The last thing he wanted to do was hesitate when a split-second decision needed to be made in the heat of a dangerous situation in order to appear politically correct, in order to *please* all the judgmental eyes just waiting for the next big cop slip-up. Such brief indecision could get you and other officers killed.

While most Portland Police cruisers featured Mobile Audio and Video (MAV) recording systems, the bureau had not yet instituted body cameras—but everyone knew they would be coming. Cameras or no cameras, Deetz was determined to teach Brandon the right way to police, and to stick to it with boldness and confidence.

As if the job didn't have enough pressure, these added land-mines would make it tough for Brandon and for any officer joining the ranks now. Not only that, but since Portland Mayor Barbara Meeks had jumped on the bandwagon to 'defund the police,' the bureau's budget had been slashed by millions and was therefore hundreds of officers short of "authorized strength," as determined by the city. Now the mayor found herself awkwardly backpedaling, requesting several million dollars in emergency "re-funding" so the police could adequately address the violence.

*A farce.*

Deetz had lost all faith in the political system.

Because of the turmoil, officers were leaving the Bureau in record numbers, with more than one-hundred-and-twenty quitting in the past nine months. Many cited low morale and burnout from nightly protests, which often escalated into physical confrontations and the massive use of teargas.

*No wonder Tidwell looks so bad.*

Even with all those negatives, Deetz was overwhelmingly proud and honored Brandon had wanted to become a law enforcement offi-cer. What more could a father ask for than to have his son consider his father a role model and a force for good? Brandon had expressed those thoughts to Deetz several times of late and it had made his heart swell with pride and satisfaction, knowing he had made a posi-tive and lasting impression on his son. And he knew his oldest son J.P., and daughter Leena, felt similarly—in their own ways.

Leena, nineteen, would always believe Deetz had hung the moon. J.P., their oldest at twenty-five, loved his dad and highly respected his career and work ethic. But J.P. and his girlfriend Tammy were more in line with the current liberal, socially minded culture, while Brandon was a red-white-and-blue conservative to the core. Hence, the brothers often butted heads about everything from gun control and police reform to politics and religion.

Deetz knew better than to broach those topics with any of them, especially J.P. and Tammy, simply because he was more conservative than they were. They would probably call him "old-fashioned" when it came to his belief in God's biblical blueprint for things like marriage, family, morals, gender, and relationships.

Anyway, Deetz and Joanie did a solid job at keeping the relationships with the kids positive, and they'd remained an extremely close-knit family, which Deetz relished—probably more than anything.

"To answer the question bluntly, no, we don't have any extra plans in place for May 7th because we don't have the budget," Tidwell said. "Fortunately, there are no big events taking place in the city this weekend, so no big crowds. Plus, we've gone about three years with no incidents. So it's business as usual."

Deetz had led the interrogation of the original shooter, Rogan Sneed, in 2018, and practically had a nervous breakdown in the process. Then he'd helped track down the copycat shooter, Daniel Bay Tinker, a year later on the one-year anniversary of the event.

"Before we hit the streets," Tidwell announced, "I want to put Wayne on the spot for a second."

Deetz instantly felt his cheeks warm.

Brandon looked over at him.

"I know Wayne is a praying man." Tidwell looked at Deetz as the room fell silent. "With your son joining the ranks, and with all the other obstacles the Bureau is facing, I thought you may want to close us out with a quick prayer or a good thought—something like that to start the week off right. And I don't want to hear any objections. If you've got a problem with prayer then just use it as a moment of silence."

*Whoa. "On the spot" was an understatement.*

Deetz looked to his left at longtime friend, Investigator Virgil Bennett, whose eyebrows were raised in rather comical anticipation. Next to Virgil, Assistant Head of Homicide Sid Sikorski sat leaning over with his head down, clutching his trademark silver mug. More close friends, Detectives Ben Briggs and Angie Cook, sat quietly to Deetz's right, each of them holding coffee cups and eyeballing Deetz.

He sat up in his chair and cleared his throat. "I was just looking around at the faces in here. Man, some of us go way back. Many of you . . . we've gone to war together. We've had each other's backs. We're like family." He fought back a flood of emotion, brought on by a mixture of the pride he felt from Brandon's first day to the nostalgic feelings of his own upcoming retirement. "Each of you have lives outside of here. You have families of your own, just like Brandon and me," Deetz said. The room was dead silent. Brandon's head was down, but his bright eyes were fixed on his dad.

"I was just sitting here thinking how much policing has changed," Deetz said. "How Brandon and others of you are stepping into something very different than many of us did, back in the day." Several officers voiced low murmurs of agreement and others snapped their fingers. "But one thing hasn't changed. And that is— our need for protection out there. So, if you will . . ." Deetz closed his eyes, leaned forward, bowed his head, and heard others shifting to do the same. "Dear God, that's what we ask of you today—to go before us and behind us. For your angels to surround us and protect us. Hem us in with your love and security. Help us make quick, efficient, wise decisions. Keep us safe."

He paused, took a deep breath, and exhaled.

"Help us fulfill the PPB mission statement," he continued, "to reduce crime, preserve life, protect property—"

The white double-doors busted open.

All heads snapped up.

Detective Wesley Fitch had burst in, out of breath, white-knuckling a police radio. His shirt was untucked, his face was red, and his eyes were the size of saucers. Deetz had never seen Fitch so undone.

"We have an active shooter," he yelled. "South Harbor Drive and Hawthorne Avenue. Two people have been hit," his voice broke, "including one of ours."

As navy uniformed bodies began to scramble all around Deetz, something about the address of the shooting kept him fixed to his chair.

"There may be multiple shooters. We're not sure yet," Fitch said loudly. "We have one active officer on the scene requesting backup."

Brandon was on his feet, coming toward Deetz, who was trying to place the address, but his mind had bleached.

Sergeant Tidwell approached Fitch in three giant strides. "Have you scrambled SERT?"

Fitch nodded. "First thing I did."

Tidwell patted Fitch's shoulder and turned toward his officers. "Sikorski will run point. Virgil will assist," he yelled. "Job one is to get the shooter or shooters. All units, go."

"Dad, come on!" Brandon got to Deetz and reached out a hand. "That's J.P.'s office."

**2**

_______

Brandon's head buzzed as he and his dad got to their Portland Police squad car—a black-and-white Ford Interceptor SUV.

"Let's stick with the plan. You drive." Deetz sounded on edge as he headed for the passenger side.

Brandon quickly got into the driver's seat and strapped in. Adrenaline pumped through his veins and ticked at his temple. "You should call J.P., make sure he's okay," he said to Deetz. "He's been working out early, before work some days. They have a gym on the second floor."

"I didn't know that." Deetz rather frantically worked his phone out of his back pocket.

"Yeah. We talked over the weekend."

Brandon started the car and backed up quickly.

"You know where you're going?" Deetz said.

"First Ave," Brandon said.

"No, go the Parkway. It'll be faster I think."

Without a word, Brandon headed for the exit of the parking lot, toward SW Naito Parkway.

Deetz fumbled with his phone, finally found J.P.'s number, and pressed it. "Did he say how early he gets in?"

Tension buzzed in the air between them.

"Just 'real early.' He said it's quiet, hardly anyone's in there. He listens to podcasts while he works out."

*Which isn't good, because he won't hear a shooter.*

"You'll get off at Lincoln," Deetz said.

"I know."

"What else do we need to do right now?" Deetz flicked his eyes down toward the illuminated panel between them.

Brandon jabbed the siren buttons.

"Good," his dad said.

*I was about to do that.*

It was weird for Brandon to see his dad in police blues again. It'd been years since he'd been on a beat. As an investigator he'd worn street clothes to work almost as far back as Brandon could remember.

Static blared on the radio, then a voice from Bureau headquarters. "One ambulance has arrived on the scene. They're working with the active officer on the ground to get to the injured parties."

Brandon clenched his teeth and felt his face warm at the thought of the cowardly shooter. He'd always been outraged at such sickening, dastardly behavior, and now he finally had a chance to *do* something about it.

A small part of him was worried about Deetz, while being concerned for himself at the same time. After all, his dad was over sixty and back out on the streets, which would be dangerous and physically demanding. Brandon was not crazy about having the stress of learning the new job, plus the responsibility of keeping track of his dad. Of course, his dad would resent that, and Brandon would never mention it, especially because it had been Deetz's idea for Brandon to ride with him during his field training, which lasted anywhere from two to six months.

But Brandon knew Deetz's mind was still sharp, that he still worked out and did his weekday run/walk like clockwork. He was in better shape than most people his age and was, in fact, trimmer than many of the younger cops on the force.

Deetz had his phone to his ear. He held a finger up and spoke. "J.P., it's your dad and brother. It's Brandon's first day on the job. We're headed toward your office complex. We have word there's an active shooter. You and your office mates need to evacuate if you safely can. If not, hide. Hunker down and lock the doors, turn off the lights. Find weapons. Be ready to attack if it should come to that."

"Dad." Brandon shook his head and slashed his throat with an index finger. "He's not going to play all that. No one plays their messages. Just hang up. He'll call you when he sees you called."

Deetz threw up his hands and spoke into the phone again. "Call me as soon as you get this. Love you." His voice trailed off, he ended the call, and clutched the phone in both hands.

"You guys talk often?" Deetz said.

"Once every couple weeks." Brandon's voice broke and he forced himself to take a couple deep breaths. The anticipation of facing an active shooter and the thought of his brother possibly being in harm's way had him wired.

"That surprises me. I'm glad you do," Deetz said.

"Yeah, he usually calls me . . . to check in."

"Be careful. Slow down just a bit. Your turn's coming up."

Brandon ignored the fact that his dad wasn't giving him a chance to act on his own and eased up on the gas slightly, watching for SW Lincoln Street. His heart tapped rapidly in the center of this chest.

"All units, this is Tidwell," came the sergeant's voice over the radio. "The shooter or shooters are now inside the Farris-Junger Office Complex at the corner of South Harbor Drive and Hawthorne Avenue. I repeat, they are *inside*. There is no gunfire on the plaza right now where the two people are down. One of the victims says the shooter works on the fourth floor. It's a nine-story building. SERT has been scrambled and will be there stat."

Brandon and Deetz glanced at each other and Brandon swallowed hard.

That was indeed J.P.'s building—and floor. He was the director of public relations for Jumpy Jim's Coffee Co., a Portland favorite, which encompassed the entire fourth floor.

SERT was the city's Special Emergency Reaction Team, fresh on Brandon's mind after having studied every aspect of the Portland Police Bureau night and day for the past sixteen weeks of Basic Academy. The team responded to critical incidents and high-risk operations such as hostage events, barricaded suspects, terrorism—

and active shooters. It'd even crossed Brandon's mind that he may want to work for SERT someday.

"The two downed bodies are on the plaza in front of the complex," Tidwell continued. "There's an empty car parked out there where it shouldn't be, with the driver door open. It could be the shooter's vehicle—a white Ford EcoSport. Approach with caution as it may be wired to detonate."

Brandon floored it down Lincoln, impressed with the power of the SUV. Deetz held onto the grab handle above his head. Brandon could tell by the creases in his dad's forehead and the rigidness of his body that he was worried about J.P.

So was he.

**3**

___________

BRANDON WAS DRIVING SO FAST, Deetz wondered if he realized their turn was coming up.

"We're almost to Hawthorne. Slow down!"

"I know, dad. Will you let me drive, please?"

The tension in the car was palpable.

Brandon made the sharp turn on what felt like two wheels and gunned the SUV. The vehicle roared down the city street, which was just coming alive with cars and pedestrians.

*He's not wasting any time getting his feet wet,* Deetz thought.

It was 7:15 a.m. Joanie would be having her coffee and quiet time at home in the same chair she had for the past twenty years. She would be sick with worry if she knew what was happening.

*Good thing she doesn't.*

Deetz purposefully calmed himself and closed his eyes. *Protect J.P. Keep us safe. Help us.*

When they got to the intersection at South Harbor Drive, Brandon swerved into the office park and headed toward the large circular drive and plaza in front of the Farris-Junger Office Complex.

"There's the white EcoSport," Deetz said.

Without hesitation, Brandon gunned the squad car directly toward two Portland police cars that were empty and parked to the right, along with two ambulances, one of which had just arrived.

SERT was not there yet and Deetz's heart swelled. That meant they would be going in first. He was more worried about Brandon and J.P. than anything.

Brandon hit the brakes and threw the SUV into park.

"Now, stay close," Deetz said, his heart thundering. "We need to stop the shooter. That's job one."

Both were out in an instant.

Two paramedics had a blond woman on a stretcher in one ambulance, and two more had just arrived and were tending to the downed male officer who was on the ground thirty yards away.

"This patient says the shooter's an employee," said a young, dark-haired female paramedic as she jumped out the back of the first ambulance wearing plastic gloves covered in blood. "Coffee company on the fourth floor."

Deetz's stomach dropped as if he'd just crested a peak on a roller coaster.

"She works there," the paramedic said. "One officer just entered the building."

Deetz wanted to jump in the ambulance and ask the patient if she knew J.P., if J.P. was inside, if J.P. was okay—but he couldn't do that.

"What else?" Deetz asked.

The paramedic shut the back doors. "She's in and out of consciousness. We were lucky to get that."

"Did she say how many shooters there are?"

"She only saw one. Sorry, gotta go. Good luck, guys." She hurried around to the driver's door, snapped off the bloody gloves, and jumped in the ambulance to drive, while her partner tended to the patient in back.

Deetz looked at Brandon.

They locked eyes and a lightning bolt of tension and valor ignited between them.

The siren from the ambulance came alive and the vehicle heaved away in a cloud of black exhaust.

Brandon clenched his teeth, looked at the building, and back at his dad.

"Ready?" Brandon said.

Deetz gave a sharp nod.

They both drew their weapons, racked the slides, and headed toward the large glass front of the building.

There was nothing they could do for their colleague who'd been shot—who was being hoisted onto a stretcher—but they may be able to prevent further loss of life if they hurried.

Deetz tried to get J.P. out of his head, telling himself he would be okay. But his son kept resurfacing to the forefront of his mind.

With guns pointing straight ahead, up at the windows, and all around—Deetz and Brandon ran for the front doors, one of which had been blown out by a gun blast leaving a five-foot opening. Broken glass was everywhere.

"Hold up, son, let me go first," Deetz said, out of breath, wondering why an employee would have to shoot his way inside?

Brandon stopped with his back to the adjacent door that was still intact, gun locked in his hands in front of his face, pointing upward.

Deetz stepped through the shattered opening and crunched through the glass toward the escalator. He smelled gunpowder and heard footsteps.

Brandon came through the door.

Deetz listened intently and looked up.

Two women, arms interlocked and whimpering, ran down the escalator with terror on their faces.

"This way!" Deetz waved them toward the front doors. "What did you see?"

One of the two, a heavy white woman slowed to talk, but her companion, a petite Hispanic lady, let go of her, ran, and ducked out the front door.

"We thought we heard shots . . . below us." She panted. "We didn't want to take any chances. We ran."

"Good! What floor were you on?" Brandon said.

"Five. What's going on?" she said.

"Active shooter. Can you tell us anymore?"

She cupped her mouth with a hand, shook her head, and burst out crying.

"Are there other people on your floor?" Deetz said.

"I . . . I don't know. I didn't see any, but there are lots of different businesses on our floor. There probably are."

"Thank you." Deetz patted her back and Brandon took her elbow and quickly guided her toward the door, then came jogging back to Deetz.

"We'll work our way up to the fourth floor on foot," Deetz said.

Brandon ran toward the elevators.

"Brandon!" Deetz called.

Brandon eyed above the elevator doors and ran back to Deetz. "One elevator is on this floor and one is on the fourth floor," he said.

"Good thinking to check that. So the shooter may have it waiting for him on four," Deetz said. "Come on. No time to waste."

Deetz ran up the escalator to the second floor and Brandon followed.

"I'll go left, you go right," Deetz said. "Take a quick glance. Maybe go thirty feet or so. If there's nothing, we take the steps to three. Watch for the gym, for J.P."

Brandon gave a breathless nod and took off.

Deetz passed the office suites of a dentist, then an ad agency. The wide, gray-carpeted hall was quiet and dark. Seeing no gym or people, he quickly headed back toward the elevators.

Brandon was not there yet, so Deetz kept going to the right where Brandon had gone.

A door swung open. Deetz pointed his gun. But it was Brandon who came through followed closely by a white male and a black female with alarm bursting from their wide eyes and gaping mouths. They were both sweating and wearing workout clothes.

"They were the only ones in the gym," Brandon said to his dad. "I'm sending them down the escalator."

"Good," Deetz said. "I'll find the stairs."

Brandon jogged to the escalator with the man and woman practically clinging to him. At the top, he stopped, checked all around, and sent them running down the steps.

"This way!" Deetz yelled.

Brandon followed his dad through a door, and they started up the stairwell steps.

"Dad," Brandon said. "J.P. was in the gym—earlier. That lady knows him. She saw him."

Deetz stopped and turned around, looking down at Brandon,

who had been behind him. He got light-headed and gripped the railing.

"He was in there earlier—this morning?" Deetz said.

Brandon nodded and kept going up the steps, past his dad. "Yeah. He worked out, showered, and left. Come on!"

"When?"

"Twenty minutes ago."

Brandon was leading now, running up the steps.

Deetz took an enormous breath and exhaled, trying to shake away the tiny white stars from his vision. He took the steps two at a time with nausea burning at the base of his throat.

He heard Brandon bust open the door to the third floor above him.

"You coming?" Brandon yelled.

"Yeah." Deetz prayed silently for strength and clarity as he raced up the next few steps to the platform on the third floor where Brandon was waiting with the door open.

"I gave a look," Brandon said, breathing hard. "Nothing's happening here. Let's get to four."

"Hold on." Deetz jogged past him and looked all around. More quiet, dim hallways.

*He's right.*

Deetz hurried back to Brandon.

"You're right. Let's go."

*Pop, pop . . . pop.*

The muffled noise came from above, along with screams.

"Gunshots! Let's go, Dad!" Brandon threw the door open for Deetz and hurled up the steps toward the fourth floor.

**4**

---

Deetz flew up the steps behind Brandon, preparing his mind to enter battle, pleading with God to keep J.P. and Brandon safe. As he ascended, fragments of the May 7, 2018, mass shooting at Pioneer Square came flying at him like shrapnel.

> *Crumpled bodies. Torn and contorted. Moaning for help. The young shooter, Rogan Sneed, saying afterward he just wanted to get as many as he could . . . The carnage from the day—and the pressure Deetz had been under to lead the interrogations—was like nothing he'd experienced in his three decades of police work.*

None of that mattered now.

He snapped his mind back to the moment.

"Brandon, wait!" he yelled.

When Deetz arrived at the door of the fourth floor, Brandon had his back against it and his gun locked in an upward position in front of him; he was breathing heavily from the climb and adrenaline. His eyes were wide and hyper-alert, his shoulders back, his body rigid.

Deetz nodded steadily, wanting to calm everything down, allow them to catch their breath, and get on the same page before they went in.

"Okay, listen to me," Deetz whispered, breathing hard, stepping closer to Brandon, and talking fast. "I'll go first. Prepare to see bodies down, bad—maybe even your brother. They may be screaming for you to help them." He shook his head and grabbed Brandon's arm. "We're going for the shooter with all we've got. SERT will be right behind us. But right now, it's us. We're not negotiating." His last words he spoke through gritted teeth. "Put him down."

"Okay, let's go." Brandon bounced as he spoke, done with the pep talk.

Deetz grabbed his radio from his shoulder and said, "This is Wayne Deetz. We're on the fourth floor where the shooter is. The coffee company. A witness saw one shooter, an employee. Brandon and I are going in."

Deetz placed his free hand on the silver bar that would open the door.

"Stay behind me till we figure out what's going on."

Deetz pushed the door open and entered with his elbows out and Glock high.

BRANDON HAD NEVER BEFORE EXPERIENCED the feelings he was having now, his mind pulsing on high alert. With his gun in front of him he followed his dad into a low-lit, plush elevator area with mirrors, large plants, and several contemporary chairs. To the left was a large, handsomely lit wall display with glass shelves featuring awards and plaques the company had accrued. To the right was a large floor-to-ceiling glass wall and door with the Jumpy Jim's Coffee Co. logo etched in the glass.

Deetz headed for the door.

Brandon followed.

Deetz opened the door as quietly as possible, but the latch made a loud metal clicking noise.

As they got inside and approached the empty receptionist's desk Brandon smelled gun smoke, then noticed a wisp of it hanging in the air in the early morning sunlight. The office lights were not on yet so there was a stark contrast of shadows and sunbeams.

"Body." Deetz nodded to his left as he made his way around the long, wood receptionist's desk with his gun trained in front of him.

The black-haired female lay on her back with gunshot wounds at her chest and thigh. Her eyes remained open in terror. She was dead.

Brandon's blood boiled. He feared for J.P.

*Bam!*

*Bam, bam, bam.*

The gunshots echoed harshly from back within the offices.

A man cried out in pain.

*This is real.*

*There is an active shooter within yards of me.*

*I'm in the middle of it.*

*This is real. This is real. Jesus help us.*

Chills engulfed Brandon. Never in his life had he been so scared and so

fuming mad at the same time.

His dad looked back at him with his mouth sealed shut and nodded slowly. Knowingly. Confidently.

His look gave Brandon assurance.

Noises came from where the shots had rung out.

A door opened and closed.

There was a shoving noise, like the sound of a heavy cabinet being moved.

"Wayne," came a pained male voice, "he's back there. He's got at least two automatics. I think I clipped him."

Deetz dashed to the floor to his right and whispered, "Danny!"

It was a Portland officer—the one who'd entered alone before them. He was pressing his lower stomach as hard as he could with both hands, but blood covered everything and was gurgling out of the wound like a spring. The shot had entered just below his ballistic vest.

Deetz leaned close to Danny's face and whispered, "Is he alone?"

The officer nodded. "I think so."

Brandon covered them as Deetz knelt over the wounded officer.

"Are there other people back there?" Deetz said.

"I only got this far." The officer shook his head feebly with a half-smile. "I got him in the shoulder, I think. He doesn't have armor."

"Good," Deetz whispered. "SERT's coming, Danny. Paramedics will be right here. Can you hang on till then?"

The officer closed his eyes, nodded, and grunted. His bottom lip quivered. "I've got to. My wife . . . my girls." Tears filled his eyes and his voice trailed off.

Brandon didn't think he was going to make it.

"We're going to get him, Danny. Hang on."

"That's your boy, isn't it?" As Danny looked up into Brandon's eyes a tear streaked down his face. His police hat lay crumpled beneath his head.

"Yeah. His first day," Deetz said.

Danny nodded at Brandon and looked like he was going to say something, but then just closed his eyes and sighed.

In that instant, Brandon wondered whether he himself would also die this day. His first minutes on the job. The shortest career in Portland Police history.

Deetz stood, looked at Brandon, and began walking back through the offices. Brandon followed, awestruck at his dad's command of the situation, which he knew was directly connected to his faith. Deetz had the most real walk with God of anyone he knew, and it was showing itself in spades.

They entered a larger area of office cubicles with maroon dividers on dark gray Berber carpet. Deetz moved quickly weaving his way right through the center of the maze without hesitation. Brandon checked each cubicle, thinking perhaps they'd find people hiding. But instead all he saw was a blur of plants, photographs of smiling people, standing desks, coffee mugs, and computers.

A phone rang near them and startled Brandon.

Both men stopped.

It was a desk phone, not a cell, from one of the cubicles.

Deetz knelt to one knee and signaled for Brandon to do the same, thinking maybe the shooter would appear.

Then they heard metal, clicking rapidly, then loud lunging.

The office phone continued to ring and Brandon wished it would stop.

"I know you're in there, Dowdy!" a male voice screamed.

Deetz instantly headed toward the voice.

With chills, Brandon followed his brave dad, mentally preparing for a gun battle.

Just then, a red-headed woman popped out of a cubicle and Brandon came within a millisecond of discharging his weapon.

She took off running with brown eyes the size of ping pong balls. Her face was blotchy and she was crying, with both hands over her mouth. Brandon nodded and pointed her toward the doors, then turned back to his dad.

**5**

———————

DEETZ WAS hyper-vigilant and felt as if he was walking two feet above the ground as he moved through the smoky haze toward the noise—toward the shooter. His blood pounded through his veins like a raging river. He was frightened, but he had a job to do.

And two sons to protect.

So *he* was on the offensive now.

*He* was the one to fear now.

*He* was the one to be dealt with, *you coward*.

He'd learned over the past thirty years, that was the attitude he had to have to survive, to overcome, to defeat the evil—the enemy.

From the rattling noise and nudging he'd heard, Deetz believed the shooter was trying to get into a locked room, perhaps where people were hiding.

*Maybe J.P.*

Deetz thought if he could sneak up on the guy from behind while he was trying to get into the room, that would be optimal.

"Dad!" Brandon whispered.

Deetz looked.

Brandon nodded to his right.

Blood on the floor.

Brandon started to follow it.

"Hey," Deetz whispered, "let me go."

Brandon gave a quick nod and Deetz followed the trail of blood into a wide, dark hallway. He got his Mag-Lite from his belt, turned it on, and held it in an icepick grip with his left hand, and crossed his Glock over the top, locking wrists.

Brandon watched his dad and did the same.

The muffled sound of sirens grew louder outside. Help was getting closer, but Deetz wanted to finish this. Once the SERT crew exploded onto the scene it would be chaos, with possible flash-bangs and lots of smoke madness.

*It'll be much cleaner to end it now.*

The shooter had yelled the name "Dowdy," which had instantly registered familiar to Deetz. It was a colleague of J.P.'s, some rich yuppie with whom J.P. had butted heads on more than one occasion.

Maybe Dowdy had fired the shooter and he was out for revenge —a sadly typical scenario these days.

Gray smoke hung in the air and filled Deetz's nose.

He glanced back at Brandon whose wide eyes flicked to meet his.

What Deetz wanted to tell Brandon was to be careful, because they could run into the shooter, or innocent bystanders like J.P., Dowdy, or their co-workers. But this was no time for words. Instead, Deetz gave Brandon a quick nod and as much of a smile as he could muster.

Deetz then followed the blood with the beam of his light up the hallway. The blood was much more than droplets; the guy was leaking substantially.

*Good.*

Deetz came to a closed door on the left where blood had pooled. He approached the door, thinking it was the one the shooter must've just rattled.

Brandon approached Deetz and covered him while Deetz pointed his Mag-Lite through a small, narrow vertical window into the dark room. Deetz spotted a long, oval conference table turned on its side.

*Someone's hiding behind it.*

*J.P.?*

Swivel chairs from the table were clustered in a group of seven or eight in front of the door. *Good.*

Whoever was in there had done the right thing and Deetz only hoped they would stay put until this was over.

He picked up the blood trail again with his Mag-Lite and began to follow it.

But noises came from the conference room he'd just left. Then the door of the room clicked open.

"Can we get out?" a man whispered. "I'm Christopher Dowdy, the CEO."

Deetz shined his light on the man who stepped from the conference room into the hallway. He had neatly combed brown hair and wore an untucked Oxford shirt with the sleeves rolled up, khaki shorts, and loafers.

"No!" Deetz hissed. "Get back in there!" He told Brandon to cover him and dashed back to the man.

"Do what you were doing. Hide." Deetz began to push the man back into the conference room and noticed movement inside.

"Dad!" J.P. stepped toward his dad from the dark room.

"J.P., thank God! Are you hurt?"

"No, we're okay."

"How many are with you in there?"

"Just us two."

"Get back in there. Lock it. Hide. Do what you were doing. He's still out here."

Deetz hoped their voices hadn't carried to the shooter.

Just as J.P. and Dowdy turned to go back into the room, a gunshot blast shattered the silence and lit up the hall like a strobe light—but from a different direction than expected.

Deetz felt as if a bullet had heated within inches of his head.

"Ahh!" one of the men next to Deetz screamed and dropped to the floor. He was hit.

Deetz was afraid it sounded like J.P.

The other man, Dowdy, stood there frozen for an instant, then dove back into the conference room to hide.

That meant J.P. was down; he'd been shot!

Deetz raised his gun and light toward where the gunshot had come from—the opposite end of the hallway, where he and Brandon had just left.

Either there was a second shooter or the one they were after had circled around.

*He knows the layout of the offices.*

Deetz's light landed on the shooter.

The scene flicked to slow motion.

He had short black hair and black glasses. A clean-cut babyface. Short-sleeve white button-down shirt, the left shoulder of which was covered in blood. Bermuda shorts. Crocs. Coming with gun pointed. Screaming for Dowdy to come out.

A flash and loud bang came from Brandon's direction.

The shooter's white shirt exploded in a splash of red.

Brandon fired a loud and echoing second shot.

Another burst of blood.

The shooter contorted and dropped.

*Dead.*

Deetz dove into the conference room with his Mag-Lite, his hands trembling.

J.P. was rolling on the floor, covering his head with both hands, blood everywhere.

But he was conscious.

He was alive.

# 6

THE WHOLE DEETZ family gathered in one of the generic waiting areas at Sisters of Charity Hospital in downtown Portland. Deetz and his wife Joanie were there along with Brandon, daughter Leena, and J.P.'s girlfriend, Tammy.

Deetz and Brandon were both still in uniform, and Brandon was in a fog. After all, he'd just killed a man on his first day of work for the Portland Police Bureau and his older brother had been shot in the head.

J.P. had been "extraordinarily lucky," according to the gruff looking ER doctor named Kilgore, who looked as if he hadn't slept in weeks. Joining them in the waiting area in light green scrubs with his gray beard stubble, wrist-bracelet tattoo, and clear-frame glasses on top of his head, he explained that the 9mm bullet from the shooter's weapon had skimmed the crown of J.P.'s head.

"We assessed the damage in ER, determined J.P. was not in imminent danger, and patched up the wound," Kilgore explained. "Unfortunately, the scrape is large enough and shaped in such a configuration that it cannot be covered with the skin currently at the site. As you know, there's not a lot of extra skin up there." Kilgore patted the top of his head, a nest of messy ash-colored hair. "In order to improve the healing process and reduce scaring, I've contacted a plastic surgeon to come in to permanently close the wound."

Kilgore gave short, abrupt answers to questions from Deetz and Joanie, apparently in a hurry to be someplace. To wrap things up, he clapped his hands and announced, "Now, J.P. is alert and he said he's eager to see all of you, especially . . . Tammy, I think he said?"

Tammy's blush was apparent, even though she was black. In Brandon's view, she was way out of J.P.'s league. Tammy was twenty-six, tall, had an amazing body, smooth skin, and a sparkling, contagious smile. Plus, she was smart, generous, and compassionate. They'd been seeing each other for several years.

Brandon wondered if he would ever find anyone even close to Tammy's caliber.

"J.P.'s surgery will be within the next hour or two," Kilgore said. "Why don't you all go in, spend maybe twenty, thirty minutes tops with him, then let him get some rest before the plastic surgeon does her magic."


J.P.'s normally thick, dark hair was gone. His head had been shaved and was wrapped in soft white bandages that encircled his chin, ears, and the top of his head. A larger mound of bandages and a cold pack covered where the wound must have been, close to the very top of his head.

J.P. looked at peace. He was tilted upright and laying back against two pillows in the bed wearing a light blue hospital gown, a bit of dark chest hair showing. The navy bedspread and white sheet were neatly folded just above his waist and his hands rested on top of the blanket, at his sides.

"Hey," J.P. said as they filed in and circled around his bed.

Joanie muttered something with great emotion and hugged him first, for a long time, and arose from the embrace with tears streaking down her cheeks. Deetz and Leena got to him next as Tammy patiently waited for the immediate family to love on him first.

Amidst all the fuss, Brandon nudged his brother's leg through the blanket and said, "Hey, dude. Looking good . . . Nice cut."

When it was finally Tammy's turn, she bent over and held J.P.'s face in her hands and kissed him. She said something softly that the others couldn't hear, and J.P. nodded, closed his brown eyes, and tried to hold back the emotions.

In that moment, the room fell silent and seemed to be shrouded in a marvelous and warm sense of thankfulness and love and unity.

It was as if words were not needed.

They were all there, together, *alive*—and they each knew at the very core of their beings that it could have been so much worse.

Any of the three men could be dead, maimed, paralyzed.

But they weren't.

Tammy sat next to J.P. on the bed with her long jean-clad legs reaching to the floor.

"Well, buddy, how are you?" Deetz said from a chair he'd pulled close to the bed, with Leena sitting on his lap.

J.P. shook his head slowly. "I'm fine. I'm wondering how bad this is?" He pointed toward the wound.

"You actually look hilarious," Leena said. "You look like you just got a tooth pulled, like in the cartoons."

Brandon snickered.

Leena was on the autism spectrum and there were never any filters with her, which often brought the family laughs (and sometimes, angst).

"They said the bullet just skimmed you," Deetz said. "So it sounds like just a flesh wound. It should be fine."

"But I mean the scar," J.P. said.

Tammy patted his hand.

Joanie said, "It's not going to be bad, honey. The plastic surgeon will make you look like new."

"Plus you've got long hair," Leena said. "It's not like you're bald, like dad."

They all laughed.

"I can't believe you guys were the first ones there," J.P. said to Deetz and Brandon.

Brandon replayed the chaotic scenes in his mind, which made him anxious just thinking about it.

"Actually, Danny Hernandez went in first," Deetz said. "He got hit . . . He didn't make it."

Brandon felt as if he'd had the wind knocked out of him. "No way," he said. "How do you know?"

"Virgil texted me."

"Who was the shooter?" J.P. said. "I never even saw him."

"Did you see Dad called you when we were on the way?" Brandon said.

"I saw he called, but I'd just finished working out down on the second floor. I was showering and getting ready for work in the locker room. I got up to our offices and heard a shot—and screams. I wanted to get out of there, but I was back in the terrace area. There was no way around him to get out. I ran into Dowdy and we decided to hide. Who was it, Dad?"

Deetz shook his head and looked at his phone. "Don't know yet. Virgil's going to let us know once they have a positive ID. A paramedic told us that a woman who'd been shot said it was a Jumpy Jim's employee. We initially thought there may be more than one shooter."

"There were two people working out when I was. Did they make it out?"

Deetz nodded. "Brandon found them. They made it."

"What about our other guy, Dad? The one hit on the plaza?" Brandon said.

"He's stable. He's going to make it," Deetz said. "I may try to see him while I'm here. You can come with me if you want."

"Who, Wayne?" said Joanie.

"Andy Grover."

"Oh, dear."

"I'll go with you," Brandon said.

Joanie walked over to Brandon, put her arms around him, and held him.

They embraced for a long time, looking at the others.

Brandon knew from her silent gesture that his mom was telling him how thankful she was that he had survived the ordeal, and possibly how sorry she was that he'd had to go through it, and to kill another human being.

Strangely, Brandon did not feel remorse about ending the life of the shooter. He guessed those feelings would come in the hours and days ahead. But for now, he was still numb and somewhat dazed.

"Whoever it was, he yelled the name Dowdy," Brandon said.

J.P. pursed his lips and chewed the inside of his lower lip, not looking at any of them.

"Haven't you had some issues with him?" Deetz said.

Tammy shifted positions uncomfortably on the bed, tilted her head at J.P. awkwardly, and put a hand on his shoulder.

The name Dowdy seemed to have hit a chord with her.

"He's my boss," J.P. said. "We don't get along."

"I thought you loved your boss," Brandon said.

"That was Jarod Jenkins. He left. He was great. Dowdy's one of the owners. He forced Jenkins to resign because he thought the company wasn't growing fast enough. I thought we were doing great. We were on a good, steady upward trajectory. Now, things are a mess. The whole morale and culture have changed."

Tammy cleared her throat and patted J.P.'s arm, as if to stop him from getting worked up.

"Dowdy's a creep. He's ruining the company," J.P. said. "I've got my resumé out. I've had it out."

Silence fell like a blanket over the room.

No one was going to verbally doubt J.P.'s decision to look elsewhere for work. But they all knew he'd always loved his job, believed in the product, and had planned to be there a long time.

"What's a resumé?" Leena said.

Everyone breathed a little easier as Joanie explained what it was to Leena.

"What'd he look like . . . the shooter?" J.P. said.

"J.P., please." Tammy stood, crossed her arms, and faced him. "Do we have to talk about this?"

"I'm just curious!"

The shooter's image was crystal clear in Brandon's mind and it still didn't seem real that he had ended the man's life.

But, again, Brandon did not regret his actions.

The man had to be stopped.

Someone had to do it.

That was his job now.

"White. Clean-cut," Brandon said. "Short black hair, black glasses. Nice shorts. Crocs. About five-ten, hundred and seventy pounds. Big watch. Looked like a computer geek."

J.P. frowned, inhaled deeply, and sighed.

With her arms still crossed, Tammy closed her eyes momentarily, turned away from J.P., and walked out of the room.

## 7

THE DOOR to the room clicked closed and everyone looked at each other.

"What's wrong with Tammy?" Deetz said to J.P. as gently as he could.

J.P.'s mouth sealed into a slit. He closed his eyes, shook his head, then pushed his head even further back on the pillows.

The reason Deetz asked was because there had never been any drama with Tammy. She was always upbeat, positive, and managed to find the silver lining in every cloud—and the good in every person. She'd studied social work and was an investigator with the Family Services Division of the Portland Police Bureau—which meant she went into residences to investigate potential domestic violence and the abuse or negligence of children and the elderly. She and J.P. also volunteered at an inner-city homeless shelter.

Tammy was a strong, beautiful young woman, the oldest of four kids from a single-parent home. Her mom, Eunice, worked three jobs and had all four kids at church every Sunday when they were growing up. Tammy was a Christian and always said she was her mom's number one fan.

With his eyes closed and his head back on the pillows, J.P. said, "Did the shooter say anything more about Dowdy? Anything specific?"

Deetz looked at Brandon and they both shook their heads.

"No." Deetz said. "Why?"

"He's a messed-up dude," J.P. said.

The room fell silent as they waited for more.

J.P. raised his head and looked at Deetz.

"I have a feeling I know who the shooter is."

"Who?" Brandon said.

"Greg Newman. He fits the description. He's our controller."

Deetz checked his phone again to see if he'd received an ID on the shooter, but he hadn't.

"Christopher Dowdy had an affair with Greg Newman's wife," J.P. said, glumly. "It ruined Newman's life, his family. Three kids. Complete mess."

"Is Dowdy married?" Joanie said.

"Oh yeah," J.P. said. "There's more dirty laundry. He has real issues. But I'm getting ahead of myself. We employ more than a hundred people. This could have been anyone."

"What's the controller do?" Brandon said.

"Pretty much manages all the cash for the company," J.P. said.

"Well, whoever it was shot everyone in his path," Brandon said. "One sick individual."

"One sick individual," Leena repeated as she stood up from Deetz's lap, walked over to J.P., and leaned her head on his chest, hugging him as he lay in the bed.

J.P. put his arms around her.

Leena closed her eyes and said, "Thank you, Jesus, that J.P. is okay."

J.P. patted her and said, "And Dad and Brandon, too."

Leena popped up and said, "You guys know the story about the ten lepers, right? Jesus healed all of them and only one came back to say thanks. Jesus was like, 'Where's everyone else I healed?'"

Deetz's phone vibrated. It was a text from Virgil. The woman hit on the plaza, Jackie Brooks, was going to live. The one shot inside the offices, Carrie Sandowski, was pronounced dead at the scene. Deetz shared the news with the family. J.P. squinted, pinched the bridge of his nose, and said with a tone of agony that he could not believe this was happening.

"Carrie was engaged," J.P. whispered, and dropped his head back on the pillows in anguish.

Gruesome visions from the gloomy aftermath of the Pioneer Square shootings of 2018 replayed in Deetz's mind. They were interrupted by a soft knock at the door.

Tammy came back in the room and crossed to Joanie. "Your pastor's here," she whispered. "I wasn't sure if I should invite him in or not."

J.P. winced and shook his head.

Pastor Scott was from Wayne and Joanie's church. It didn't surprise Deetz that he'd shown up. Although he had a large congregation and was pushing sixty, he had the energy of a twenty-five-year-old and kept his thumb on the pulse of everything and everyone at the church.

"Thanks, sweetie." Joanie rubbed Tammy's back for a moment. "I'll go talk to him. J.P. how about some fruit or something to eat? I can see what I can find."

"They said no food before the surgery," he said. "I really don't want to see anyone else, guys. I'm beat."

"Okay. Right. You need to rest." Deetz went over and put a hand on J.P.'s shoulder. "We love you, buddy. We'll get out of your hair now—"

"Oh, LOL . . . good one dad!" Leena laughed hysterically. "Did you guys get that? You see what he did there? Who says Dad doesn't have a sense of humor?"

They all chuckled and even J.P. smiled as the family said their goodbyes and began to head for the door.

Two very loud knocks and the door burst open.

In came the man J.P. had hidden with at their offices that morning.

His shiny brownish blond hair was combed neatly over his tanned forehead and a big silver Bluetooth earpiece was plugged into one ear. There was a spatter of blood on the shoulder of his light blue Oxford shirt, which was still untucked with the sleeves rolled up. His khaki shorts were wrinkled and he held a huge soft drink cup in one hand. He wore shiny formal brown loafers with no socks, a look Deetz abhorred.

"Hey, hey. Wow, look at this crowd." His voice was deep and loud.

*Too loud for a hospital.*

He stuck a hand out toward Deetz. "Christopher Dowdy, J.P.'s boss. You must be J.P.'s old man."

Deetz hesitantly shook the man's hand, which was wet, and Dowdy moved on to Tammy.

"And here she is, my favorite woman on the planet—besides my lovely bride." Dowdy went to hug Tammy, but she put her hands up and backed away several steps.

Deetz couldn't believe it. Tammy had reacted like a dog that had been beat too much.

Dowdy ignored Tammy's expression of distaste, shook both of her raised hands, and turned to Joanie.

"My goodness." Dowdy stared at Joanie exaggeratedly, then whipped around and looked at J.P. "This can't be your mom." He dramatically turned back to Joanie. "She could be your wife, J.P.! It's great to meet you, Mrs. Deetz. Christopher Dowdy."

Joanie nodded at him with a manufactured smile that Deetz rarely saw from her. "Joanie," she said, and shook his hand because he insisted.

"This has been a heck of a way to start the week, huh?" Dowdy made a shivering sound and stuck a hand toward Brandon, who shook it with a questioning look on his face. "I can't believe we had all the Deetz men on the scene. What kind of a coincidence is that? You two in blue were *amazing*. Man," he pointed a gun-shaped hand at Brandon, "you were like John Wick in there. Bam, bam, bam. No hesitation whatsoever." He threw in several expletives to emphasize his point.

Joanie scowled at his language, reached out, took Leena's hand, and led her toward the door.

It was interesting Dowdy had completely ignored Leena.

"I'm Leena, FYI," she said as Joanie led her out of the room.

Deetz knew Leena was being sarcastic because Dowdy had ignored her. In fact, Deetz was surprised Leena hadn't repeated something negative J.P. had said earlier about Dowdy or chastised him for his bad language. She probably would have, but Joanie had swept her out of there fast.

"Man, how are you doing?" Dowdy held up a fist and J.P. gently bumped it.

"Not bad. Waiting on a plastic surgeon."

"Oh, wow. They've got more to do? Hey, you should have them give you a little chin lift while they're in there—get rid of some of that baby fat." Dowdy laughed at his own joke.

When no one else laughed, he changed his tone.

"Seriously, you were lucky, bro. We both were. The gods were looking out for us." Dowdy looked back and forth at Deetz and Brandon. "Do we know who it was yet?"

Deetz glanced at his phone. "Not yet."

Tammy, who'd been standing in the corner, went over to the bed, kissed J.P.'s forehead, and whispered, "I'll see you soon."

With Dowdy standing there like the elephant in the room it made for an unpleasant and guarded "goodbye" between the two. Tammy squeezed J.P.'s hand and quietly left.

"Did you guys get a good look at him?" Dowdy said.

Brandon looked at Deetz and was probably wondering if they should divulge a description to this loose cannon.

"It was dark. Lots of smoke," Deetz said. "We'll find out soon."

"I have my suspicions," Dowdy said, almost more to himself than to Deetz and Brandon. "We had to let Greg Newman go last Friday."

"What?" J.P. squawked. "Why? He's been with us since the start."

Dowdy slurped his drink. "He was questioning everything, J.P. The guy's a pain in the—" A red light flashed on his earpiece. "Oh wait, hold on a second. I've got to take this."

Dowdy tapped his Bluetooth earpiece and spoke to the caller, "Yeah." He turned his back on the others. "Okay, that's not gonna happen. What about Bucks-Hawks?" He paced. "No good. What about Phoenix, who're they playing? Spread? Who's home?" Silence. "What's the over-under on that one?" He turned around, looked at Deetz, raised his eyebrows up and down, and paced some more. "Okay, give me 'under' on the Suns' game. And Victor—give me the Dodgers again. Right . . . Later."

Dowdy clicked the earpiece to end the call and said, "Sorry gents. Where were we?"

"You were saying why you fired Newman," Brandon said evenly.

"Yeah, the last straw was when he stopped a payment to our

bean provider in Indonesia—without asking anyone. Without consulting me!"

"I thought we agreed we weren't buying from them anymore," J.P. said.

Dowdy shook his head and combed his hair over. "They're the cheapest beans out there that meet our standards."

"They *don't* meet our standards. We've been through this, Chris. That stuff is too harsh. We're trying to build a brand, not pinch pennies."

Deetz raised a hand. "Take it easy, J.P. You're supposed to be resting. We don't need you getting all worked up."

"Who is he to stop a payment, for whatever reason?" Dowdy said. "I'm the owner of the company." He cussed.

"He cares about the product—and our reputation. And you're not the only owner."

Dowdy shrugged and waved a hand. "Yeah, and I care about making a profit and keeping the company alive. No one else thinks about that. All you tree-huggers care about is your organic beans and recyclable packaging. You don't think about the bottom line. You've got no business sense. No common sense for that matter."

"Hey!" Brandon stepped toward Dowdy. "Why don't you cool it, man? This is no place for this. J.P. doesn't need to be talking business now."

Deetz's eyes burned into Dowdy to emphasize the point, but he put a hand up to stop Brandon from getting any closer to the guy.

"When you fired this Newman guy Friday, did you take his key to the building? Did he have one?" Deetz said.

"Sure did. He cleared everything out." Dowdy looked at Brandon, then Deetz. "Look, I won't keep you boys any longer." He faced J.P. "I just wanted to check on you. These are small matters compared to what happened today, right? I'll get out of your way."

Dowdy nodded at J.P., gave a thumbs-up, and said, "Good luck with the chin tuck."

J.P. only half acknowledged him.

Dowdy smacked his big drink on J.P.'s tray next to the bed and was at the door in several giant strides.

"Peace-out, Deetzes. See you tomorrow, J.P."

**8**

———

"HE EXPECTS you back to work tomorrow?" Brandon said. "What's that dude on, anyway?"

"He didn't come to check on me," J.P. mumbled. "He wants to know who the shooter is. He's scared of something. I'm telling you, he's a weasel."

"No wonder you have your resumé out. I could never work for a creep like that," Brandon said.

Deetz was looking intently at his phone.

There was a knock at the door and Dr. Kilgore entered. "Okay, all guests out. J.P. needs some peace and quiet before his surgery."

Brandon went over and fist-bumped J.P. "See you on the flipside, bro."

"I'm going to check your vitals really quick." Kilgore put on his stethoscope and began listening to J.P.'s breathing.

Deetz crossed over, bent down, and kissed J.P.'s forehead. "See you soon, pal. All will be well."


BRANDON AND DEETZ got back to the waiting area to find Pastor Scott at the center of a deep discussion with Sergeant Dolby Tidwell and Investigator Virgil Bennett, both of whom towered over the small pastor. Joanie, Tammy, and Leena sat near them snacking on fruit and crackers.

When the men saw Brandon and Deetz they stopped talking and approached them. They all shook hands and embraced. Even though Brandon was brand new to the job, he sensed a camaraderie with the officers that he had never experienced before. It was deeply satisfying.

"You guys okay?" Tidwell said.

Brandon and Deetz said they were and talked briefly about the morning's events.

"Heck of a first day." Virgil patted Brandon on the shoulder.

"Yes, it has been," Brandon said.

"He did well." Deetz looked into Brandon's eyes. "Really well. Thank God."

They briefly discussed the people who'd been injured and killed that morning and agreed they would each make a point to visit Officer Andy Grover, who was recovering on the fifth floor.

"Brandon—and Wayne, of course—we have a counselor available to you. Her name's Terri Wallender," Tidwell said. "I don't have her card with me, but I think it would be a good idea for you to set up a time to talk with her—about today."

Virgil had dug into his wallet and handed Brandon the doctor's business card.

"You get free sessions, funded by the EAP," Tidwell said.

Brandon knew from his recent Academy studies the EAP was the Employee Assistance Program. It was a nice gesture, but he didn't need counseling.

"I know you may not think you need it," Tidwell read his mind, "but I've found over the years that this type of counseling in the early stages after a traumatic event can really help."

"Yes, sir," Brandon said, wondering if Tidwell would actually follow up with him to see if he took his advice.

"How's J.P.?" Pastor Scott said.

Deetz nodded. "He seems good. Just needs a little plastic surgery and he'll be on the mend."

Leena came over to the group of men with several apples and bananas. "Excuse me," she said. "Would any of you care for some fruit?"

Joanie and Tammy smiled at the men from a nearby couch.

The men all made a big deal over Leena. Brandon took a banana and Deetz and Pastor Scott took apples.

When Leena and Pastor Scott went back to talk to Joanie and Tammy, Tidwell asked Deetz and Brandon if J.P. had been able to give them any more details about the shooter's background.

"Wait, have we ID'd him?" Brandon said, feeling left out of the loop.

Tidwell and Virgil looked at Deetz.

"Oh, yeah. Sorry, son. Virgil texted me, but we were in with J.P. and the doc. I didn't want to stress J.P. out anymore before his surgery. It was indeed Gregory Newman."

"J.P. was right," Brandon said.

Deetz and Brandon explained to the others that J.P.'s boss, Christopher Dowdy, was said to have had an affair with Greg Newman's wife, and that Dowdy fired Newman just three days earlier for going over his head to stop a payment to a coffee bean supplier.

"J.P. and Dowdy both suspected Newman," Deetz said.

"So, are you convinced this had nothing to do with the Pioneer Square shootings?" Tidwell said. "No connection?"

"So far, no," Deetz said. "I don't think they're connected."

"J.P. implied that Dowdy has more dirty laundry," Brandon said.

Deetz winced for a split-second and Brandon wondered if he should have said that.

"Like what?" Tidwell said.

Brandon looked at Deetz and kept his mouth shut, since he seemed to have said too much already.

"We don't know," Deetz said. "Dowdy apparently fired J.P.'s former boss, a guy named Jenkins, because the company wasn't growing fast enough for him. And J.P. did imply that some other things may be going on with Dowdy."

"That name sounds familiar," Virgil said.

"Dowdy?" Deetz said.

"Yeah."

"You thinking of Alexander Dowdy? The big investor-entrepreneur?" Tidwell said.

"That's it," Virgil said. "He's been in and out of the courts and headlines for years. Is he in prison?" Virgil began to search on his phone.

"I don't think he's ever done time," Tidwell said. "He's been accused of all kinds of things—here, Washington, Colorado, Nevada—but they've never nailed him on anything. Untouchable. Portland native. I think he still lives here. But, he's invested in horse racing tracks, casinos—the last thing I heard was he was dumping millions into a company in Colorado that makes marijuana drinks. They infuse cannabis into wine, tea, soft drinks."

"That's gonna be a massive industry," Brandon said.

"That's him." Virgil held up his phone and looked right back at it. "Christopher Dowdy is the son of Alexander Dowdy, who this story calls 'a driven, no-nonsense visionary, extravagant spender, and carefree playboy.' It also says he's struggled with debt and filed for bankruptcy once."

"Okay, so let's sum it up," Tidwell said. "Gregory Newman is mad because Christopher Dowdy had an affair with his wife. How long ago was that?"

Deetz shook his head. "Don't know yet."

"Okay, so then Newman stops payment on something and Dowdy fires him last Friday." Tidwell put his hands on his waist and set his shoulders back. "Newman comes in today and shoots up the place, looking for Dowdy."

Everyone seemed in agreement.

"I know it seems opened-and-closed, but I want you to be the lead investigator on it, Wayne," Tidwell said. "Brandon can help you. Just do it in uniform. I just want to make sure we confirm the shooter acted alone and there are no ties to the Pioneer Square events. And then, if there's anything we need to know about this Dowdy guy, if he's breaking the law, we need to find it. It's not gonna take all your time, so go about your beat otherwise. Is that all clear?"

"Yes, sir." Brandon looked at his dad, excited he was going to get to work a big investigation right off the bat.

But Deetz only nodded silently and looked away.

Brandon knew his dad—and he knew he didn't want to work this case.

**9**

It was all arranged for 1:30 p.m.

Deetz and Brandon, still in uniform, were on their way to interview the shooter's wife, Jessica Newman. Brandon was driving the Interceptor, finishing the banana Leena had given him.

The newly widowed Jessica Newman lived in a suburban neighborhood southwest of the city, toward Vermont Hills.

In some ways, Deetz was glad Brandon would get to work the case; he would certainly learn a lot. But in many more ways, he was troubled they'd been asked to do so. Deetz had spent the past several months preparing to go back on beat with Brandon. Mentally, he was done with investigation work. It was taxing because it required tons of research, interviews, and brainpower—and often involved late nights and weekends. It was pressure-packed because the Bureau was counting on you to get results.

Deetz had not liked the countenance of Christopher Dowdy. He seemed boisterous and careless, the type who was overcompensating. Something about the man was just plain bad blood, and Deetz really didn't want to be the one to have to delve into it.

"You want me to run through McDonald's?" Brandon said. "We probably won't get to eat till later this afternoon or dinner."

"We don't have time," Deetz said. "I'm good. Thanks."

"Well then you better eat that apple. You need something."

Deetz bit into the apple Leena had given him and agreed with a mouthful.

"You don't seem too excited about this investigation," Brandon said.

The windows in the SUV were down halfway. It was a cool sixty degrees and partly sunny. Deetz stared out his window at the large trees and homes along the way. They were almost to the Newman's place.

"It'll be fine. I was just really excited to be back on beat with you. In my mind, that's how I was going to go out. I'm over the investigation work. I'm just sick of it."

"We'll still be on beat. I mean, like Tidwell said, it should be pretty opened-and-closed, right? Do you think it will?"

"Not sure. Depends if this Dowdy character is hiding anything. Tidwell has a habit of oversimplifying things."

Brandon checked the GPS and made a turn into a neighborhood near Gabriel Park.

"This is pretty cool. I get to see you do your thing," Brandon said. "Here it is already."

He swung the Interceptor into a short blacktop driveway and parked. It was a white, two-story home with lots of huge trees and many shrubs in front. There were splotches of mold on the siding and roof, probably because of all the rain and lack of sunlight. A new-looking basketball hoop was stationed at the end of the driveway by the house. The garage door was closed.

As they approached the house, a local TV news truck pulled down the quiet street and eased to a stop in the grass along the front of the residence.

"Look who's here," Brandon said.

"Come on. Let's get in there before they corner us," Deetz said.

They quickly went up the sidewalk to the front porch and Deetz rang the doorbell. It opened almost instantly.

A blond woman of about thirty-five opened the front door while holding a young boy in her arms. He was about two with bright red cheeks and was clutching and slobbering on a toy truck. She wore gray sweatpants and an orange, unbuttoned and untucked long-sleeve shirt with the sleeves rolled up and a white tank-top beneath it. Her hair was frizzy and shoulder length. Her eyes were a pretty blue and her eyebrows were dark. She had been crying and held a tissue in one fist, along with a folded piece of paper.

Deetz introduced himself and Brandon, then confirmed the woman's name was Jessica, and that she'd been married to the shooter, Gregory Newman. The boy, who she'd sent to the other room to continue watching TV, was Daniel. Two other children a bit older than Daniel had been picked up from school by Jessica's sister and were at her home nearby, Jessica said.

The house was clean and bright. Framed family photos filled the mantel above the simple fireplace. In the center was a picture of Jessica and Gregory on their wedding day; all smiles. A dark gray cat with yellow eyes came out from around the corner, stopped, and looked up at the uniformed men. Brandon reached down to pet it and it dashed away.

On their way into the living room Deetz said, "I should tell you before we get started that my son, J.P., works at Jumpy Jim's. He knew your husband."

"I recognized your last name," Jessica said somberly. "I met J.P. at one of the company gatherings. He seemed nice. Gregory liked him, I know that."

Deetz didn't intend to go off on a rabbit trail and tell Jessica that J.P. had been in the office that morning and had actually been shot by her husband. Instead, he and Brandon took a seat on a couch near a bay window. Jessica offered them something to drink and when they said no, she moved a red plastic dinosaur toy out of an upholstered chair that was situated next to them and sat down with a sigh.

"When is the last time you saw your husband?" Deetz wrote the date and time on a small pad and prepared to take notes.

"This morning. Early. I thought he was going to work, like usual. He didn't tell me he'd been fired. I only found out a few minutes ago from my sister—she heard it on the news."

Deetz tried not to show his surprise that Gregory Newman's firing was already public. He wondered how it had gotten out so soon.

"Did anything seem out of order with Gregory this morning, different than normal?"

"Not really." She shook her head quickly and wiped below each eye with the tissue. "We haven't been on good terms anyway lately, so . . ."

"So, there's been tension between you?"

She nodded, crossed her arms, and sighed with her bottom lip quivering.

"Can you tell us why that is? What's been going on in his life that might have caused him to do this?"

Jessica's head dropped and she cried. She put a fist to her mouth to stop. "I had an affair with a man named Christopher Dowdy where he works. It's his boss. One of the owners of the company." She looked up at Deetz. "It never should've happened." She cried more but kept going. "It was a one-time thing. I know, that's what they all say, right? But I'm really not that kind of person. I still can't believe it happened . . . that I let it happen."

Deetz was about to ask another question, but she continued.

"Dowdy never liked Gregory from the start. He accused Greg of being too rigid about budgets and expense accounts. But Greg was just a meticulous person. He was dedicated. He did everything by the book. He was such a hard worker." She broke down again. "I can't believe we went all weekend and I didn't know he'd been fired. I could have helped him . . . talked through it."

Brandon got up quietly and retrieved a box of tissues that was sitting in a nearby chair, handed it to her, and sat back down. She thanked him, took a fresh tissue, and went on.

"Dowdy came onto me once at a company party—I mean strong. He was physically touching me. He'd had too much to drink. I got away from him, but Greg saw it. When it happened, later, the affair, I know now it was Dowdy's way of ruining us."

She held up a finger. "Excuse me." She blew her nose, snatched another tissue, and went on.

"When the affair was over, Dowdy leaked it around the office. Then he dropped me cold as if it had never happened, like I didn't exist. I let it happen. I admit that. But what I'm saying is, Dowdy did it to *spite* Greg. I'm sure of it. I mean, look at me!" She cried. "I know I'm overweight. I know it sounds farfetched, but Dowdy's a wicked conniver. He gets to know peoples' personalities—and he plays them. He knew an affair with me would ruin our marriage because he knew Greg was a worrier and that he tends to be para-noid. Dowdy knew Greg would never get over my infidelity. Again, I know that sounds insane, but that's how Christopher Dowdy operates."

"And he was right? Your husband did not get over the affair?" Deetz said.

"No. He didn't." With that, Jessica stuck out the hand that was holding the folded piece of white paper.

Deetz took it, unfolded it, and held it out so Brandon could read at the same time.

*Dear Jessica,*

*Ever since the day we met, you have been my world and the reason for my existence. I thought we were so happy.*

*As you know, I could not recover from the affair. I'm sorry, I tried. But the trust was gone. It was never coming back.*

*There is evil in this world, Jess. It came for you and now it's come for me. I think it comes for all people. I'm sorry it got the best of me. I'm sorry for the events of today.*

*I hope you will find someone who can help you rise above the evil and teach our children to do the same.*

*Please forget me now.*
*Gregory*

Deetz looked at Brandon, who nodded to show he had finished reading.

Deetz sighed and shook his head.

"I'm sorry, Mrs. Newman. This is tragic."

After an awkward moment of silence, Deetz said, "If you don't mind, I need to take a photo of this."

He did so, put his phone away, and handed the letter back to her.

She took it, crumpled it in her lap, and blubbered something Deetz didn't understand.

"Your husband had several guns with him this morning. What do you know about those?" Deetz said.

"Nothing!" She threw up both hands with fingers splayed and a look of anguish on her splotchy face. "This whole thing is so unlike Greg. He's a numbers guy. A geek. A nerd. I had no idea he knew anything about *guns*. I honestly don't think he had them in the house. He wouldn't do that, with the kids here. He just wouldn't."

"I will give you a heads-up, Jessica, that one or two people from our team are going to be here today—to look through Greg's things. They may even confiscate items, but you'll get them back," Deetz explained.

"I tried to look at his laptop, earlier, but it requires a fingerprint to get in," Jessica said.

"Our people will be able to bypass that."

"What about his phone? Do you know if he had it with him when . . ."

"I don't know, but our team will find out."

Brandon spoke up. "We understand your husband stopped a payment to a coffee bean supplier in Indonesia. Do you know anything about that?"

Deetz quickly added, "We believe that may be one of the reasons Dowdy fired Greg last week."

"I don't know about that, specifically, but . . . look, the former boss, Jarod Jenkins, and the other owner, Will Tomason, and most everyone who's worked there from the start—they're all about having a truly superior product. They support green initiatives, social justice, giving back to the community—all that. But when Dowdy took over, everything changed, almost overnight. His dad got involved and it's become all about the profits. A lot of people have left. Dowdy forced people out who wouldn't change their ways, like Jenkins. Greg was beside himself. He was miserable."

"How long ago was it that Jenkins resigned and Dowdy took over?" Deetz said.

"Resign. Ha! That was all smoke and mirrors. Dowdy fired him. They called it a resignation so Jenkins could find another job."

"And how long ago was it?"

"Somewhere around late spring, early fall."

"Did Gregory have substance abuse problems, Mrs. Newman?" Deetz said.

"No. No way."

"What about mental health disorders?"

Jessica's shoulders slumped, her head dropped, and she sighed audibly. Then she sat up and faced them, her eyes glistening with puddles of tears. She nodded slowly and wiped her eyes before speaking softly. "Depression runs in his family. His father committed suicide when Greg was only sixteen. He's always battled it. And anxiety. And paranoia."

"Did he seek professional help?" Deetz said.

"Of course. My gosh, over the years, he's seen a dozen doctors, psychiatrists, you name it. The last one diagnosed him with PPD, paranoid personality disorder. It's a condition in people who have a long-term distrust or suspicion of others, but it's not a full-blown psychotic disorder like schizophrenia."

"He was on meds?"

"He's been on something as long as I've known him. But there've been problems with side effects. The latest thing he was trying, he absolutely hated. He was hearing voices. Said it made him feel like he'd had a lobotomy. He was threatening to stop taking it. He may have, I don't know. I didn't keep track of that stuff."

"And you had no knowledge of what Greg planned to do today?" Deetz said soberly.

"No." Jessica stared at Deetz in silence for a moment. "But I heard him—talking to himself. Several times. It was almost like he was arguing back and forth. This one time he spoke with a voice I didn't even recognize. It was scary." She cried and put a fist to her mouth. "He mentioned Dowdy, but I couldn't understand what he was saying . . . I should have *done* something." She broke down and sobbed.

The doorbell rang.

Jessica began to stand, but Deetz held up a hand for her to stop. "It's probably reporters. We saw them park out front. Brandon, please tell them we're interviewing her and she has no comment. Tell them to stay off the property."

"Excuse me." Brandon got up and went to the front door.

"I need to tell you something else," Jessica whispered. "It involves your son, J.P."

**10**

———————

WHEN BRANDON GOT to the foyer, the little boy, Daniel, was clutching a green stuffed Kermit toy in his arms and peering up at someone through the narrow vertical window next to the front door.

"Hey buddy, who's there?" Brandon said as he approached.

The boy pointed up at whoever was outside.

"Okay, step back a minute. I'm going to see who it is." Brandon looked out the window the boy had been looking through. The boy padded off in his bare feet.

A pretty, young Asian reporter in a red dress stood there holding a KOIN news microphone. Behind her was a tall bearded guy holding an expensive-looking camera with a lighting element on top.

Brandon took a deep breath, exhaled, opened the door, stepped out, and closed it behind him.

The cameraman's light popped on like a magic trick and he pointed the camera at Brandon.

"Hi officer . . . Deetz." She read his name badge. "I'm Amanda Kim with KOIN News, and this is Adam. Can you tell us if Jessica Newman is home?"

Brandon was slightly taken aback that they were actually filming.

"She is, but she's being interviewed by us right now, Portland Police," Brandon said. "She's not talking to the media at this time."

"What's her reaction been to the tragic shooting this morning at Jumpy Jim's headquarters?" Amanda pushed the microphone close to Brandon's mouth.

Brandon felt sorry for Jessica and he didn't want people to judge her by her husband's actions. He wanted to help her.

"She's naturally extremely sad and . . . distraught."

"Of course, of course," Amanda said, almost surprised Brandon was answering. "Did Gregory Newman have mental illness, do you know?"

"He did . . . Uh, depression ran in his family. He was having it treated though."

"I see. And did Mrs. Newman have any knowledge that her husband was planning to do what he did this morning at that office building?"

The front door opened.

It was Deetz. He glared at Brandon and threw up a questioning hand as if to say, "What's going on?"

"Uh, no more comment right now." Brandon nervously turned and started back inside, glancing at a still-glaring Deetz. "Oh, and please stay off the Newman's property."

"Mrs. Newman will let you know if she has a statement," Deetz added as he got Brandon back inside and shut the door.

"How much did you say to them?" Deetz fumed. "There should have been no comment whatsoever."

"Just that she's sad," Brandon said.

Deetz shook his head exaggeratedly. "No, son. No! No comment means no comment! Did you say anything else?"

"Just about his depression—"

Deetz blew a gasket. "Brandon!"

"Dad, she—"

"Yeah, they have a way of getting people to talk. That's what they do. That's what they're good at. You have to realize what they can do with *anything* we say, Brandon. It can instantly become *world* news."

Brandon felt sick. He shook his head, replaying what he'd told her.

Deetz sighed and patted his back. "It's okay. Just learn from it. From now on it's a straight 'No comment.' That's it. You have to be cold. You'll learn. C'mon. She has something more to say."

Brandon followed Deetz back into the living room where Jessica was seated in the same chair, staring at the fireplace.

*What a mess her life is going to be. The widow of an 'active shooter.' And her kids—this will haunt them their entire lives.*

"You were starting to say something about J.P." Deetz sat back down on the couch and Brandon joined him.

"Gregory had discovered things." Jessica spoke like a robot in a trance, still staring at the fireplace. "In working closely with the company finances and local banks, Greg found out Christopher Dowdy was in debt—a lot of it."

"Personally, or as a company?" Deetz said.

"Personal. And Greg thought he might be trying to steal company funds to pay-off the debts." She shook her head and tented her hands in front of her face.

"How much debt?" Deetz said.

She turned to face him. "Thousands . . . I'm not sure."

"Whoa," Brandon said.

Deetz looked at him with his mouth sealed shut and gave an almost unnoticeable shake of his head.

That meant Brandon shouldn't have commented.

*Dang it.*

"Did Gregory find out what all the debt was for?" Deetz said.

She nodded. "He believed most of it was from gambling. What am I mincing words for? He *knew* it was from gambling—because he got threatened."

"Your husband? By whom?" Deetz said.

"He thought it was some kind of organized crime group." She laughed almost like a mad woman. "I didn't believe him! I thought he was just being paranoid. But then he showed me a text he got. They wanted him to withdraw company funds to pay them, the Mob did. The text was threatening."

"How so?"

"It mentioned me, by name." She sniffed, inhaled deeply, and wiped her nose. "Whoever wrote it knew we had three kids.

Nothing specific, but obviously dark and threatening. Greg should've called the police."

"How does J.P. fit into all this?" Brandon said.

"I told Greg he needed to talk to someone high up in the company, to tell someone what was going on with Dowdy," Jessica said. "He confided in J.P."

"I see. So J.P. knows most of what you've told us today?"

"I'm not sure how much Greg told him. He just said he finally talked to J.P. I wouldn't let up until he spoke to someone."

Deetz and Brandon needed to talk to J.P. as soon as he got out of surgery.

Jessica began to cry again, stood, and walked to a back window. After looking out for a few seconds she turned to face them.

"Greg liked J.P. He always said what a good guy he was—what a good person. He didn't say that about many people. He was very . . . untrusting." She sobbed. "I just wish someone like J.P. could have helped him . . . gotten through to him somehow."

Her phone vibrated. She worked it out of her pocket, looked at it, and her shoulders slumped. She looked at them. "I've got to take this. It's the morgue."

**11**

—————

Deetz watched TV in the family room while Joanie and Leena made dinner and set the table. He'd offered to help, but they insisted they didn't need him. So, he'd changed out of his uniform into jeans and a T-shirt and was lying on the couch with the remote, switching from news channel to news channel to review coverage of the morning events from J.P.'s office building.

Deetz and Brandon had spent the rest of the afternoon filling out paperwork at police headquarters about the Gregory Newman shootings. Deetz had to laugh at how shocked Brandon had been about all the paperwork they had to do. Deetz had walked him through it and they knocked off at five. The current schedule had them working four ten-hour days in a row, followed by three days off. Deetz doubted the days off would happen now that he'd been assigned to investigate the Gregory Newman ordeal.

They'd gone their separate ways after work, Brandon to his apartment and Deetz to the house. The smell of spaghetti sauce filled the downstairs. Deetz closed his eyes and thought he may fall asleep. Italian music came on in the kitchen. He smiled.

"How do you like that, Dad? Just like an Italian restaurant." Leena came into the family room with a kitchen towel draped over her shoulder.

"Wonderful," Deetz said.

"You want a rundown of the menu?" she said.

"Love it."

"Mom's homemade meatballs."

"Oh, you got me right there."

"Mom's homemade garlic toast."

"Oh!" Deetz moaned.

"Mom's choice of noodles. They're those green veggie ones. I can't stand them. I don't see why we can't eat normal noodles like everyone else. I can't remember the last time we had white noodles."

"Oh, come on, kid. The veggie ones are fine. They're good for you."

Leena shook her head. "I'm just having meatballs and garlic toast. Mom said it's okay."

"Nope. You must-a have-a the veg-et-able noodles!" Deetz kidded her with a thick Italian accent.

"No!" Leena yelled, ran over, and tickled Deetz.

She was strong and knew he was especially ticklish under the pits.

He got to laughing so hard he was crying.

After a minute, she stood up, out of breath. "You actually have tears, Dad."

"Ahh! I needed a good laugh. Thanks, sweetie."

"Any time, Pops."

"Dinner in five," Joanie yelled.

"Copy that?" Leena said.

"Copy." Deetz sat up on the couch and switched channels as Leena went back to the kitchen.

He looked at the TV and did a double-take. It was Brandon, talking to the KOIN reporter outside the Newman house from that afternoon.

*Uh oh.*

"Guys!" Deetz yelled. "Come quick, Brandon's on TV!"

Joanie and Leena ran in, stopped, and stared at the TV just as the reporter asked Brandon what Jessica Newman's reaction had been to the shooting at Jumpy Jim's.

"I can't get my head around this!" Leena said dramatically.

"Shhh," Joanie said.

"She's naturally extremely sad and . . . distraught," Brandon said.

"Of course, of course," the reporter said. "Did Gregory Newman have mental illness, do you know?"

"He did . . . Uh, depression ran in his family. He was having it treated though."

*No, no, no.*

Joanie's head swiveled toward Deetz. "Should he be saying that?"

"No. Shh." Deetz put a finger to his lips so he could hear the rest. As the reporter asked Brandon if Jessica had any prior knowledge about what Greg Newman had planned to do, Deetz himself was shown walking out the front door.

"There's Dad!" Leena said. "Ew, you look mad! Brandon's in tro-uble."

Joanie started asking a question and the picture on the TV switched and Deetz heard the anchor mention Christopher Dowdy.

"Hold up!" Deetz stood and glared at the TV.

It was Dowdy, being interviewed by the same reporter, apparently later that afternoon. He'd changed shirts but was still wearing the big silver Bluetooth earpiece.

"I had no idea this employee had mental health issues," Dowdy said loudly. "If we'd known, we certainly would have gotten him professional help."

Deetz felt sick. It was Brandon's interview that had led to this line of questioning.

He was also suspicious, because Dowdy appeared to be lying. Jessica Newman had just told them Dowdy knew Gregory Newman struggled with depression, anxiety, and paranoia.

"The mental health problems in our country are rampant," Dowdy continued, "and I believe we all need to do our part to recognize the symptoms and get people the help they need."

"Is it true Gregory Newman, the shooter, was fired from your company last week?" the reporter asked.

Dowdy rolled his head and eyes. "I don't want to talk about that."

"What can you tell us about Gregory Newman?"

Dowdy rocked his head back and forth before answering. "What can I say? He was obviously a very sick individual. That's the bottom line. I'm sorry for his family. But I'd rather talk about Carrie Sandowski, the brave employee we lost today, and Jackie Brooks, the other courageous employee who, fortunately, will survive. I also want to thank the fearless officers from the Portland Police Bureau who stopped the event before it got worse."

Deetz's phone rang.

He knew it would be Tidwell before he even looked at the screen.

It was.

He glanced at Joanie. "I've got to take this."

"But dinner's ready," she said.

"It's Tidwell. You guys go ahead. I'll be right there."

Joanie shot him an exasperated look and headed for the kitchen.

"Bad move." Leena said to her dad as she followed her mom.

Deetz answered the call.

"Is that the way we train new officers now?" Tidwell blared. "Teach them to blab to the media like long-lost relatives?"

"I told him to say, 'no comment,' but . . . I don't know, I think he felt sorry for Newman's wife. I'm not sure what happened, but it won't happen again, Sarge. Sorry."

"I'm not even going to get into all the repercussions that could come from this," Tidwell said. "You know, Wayne!" He cussed.

"I know. I'm sorry. I should've handled it myself. But he knows now."

"He better. That's on you." After what seemed like a minute of silence, Tidwell said, "Did you ever get up to see Andy Grover?"

"Not yet. We had to do the interview with Newman's wife. Why? Is he okay?"

"He'll be fine. But he mentioned something Newman said that I want you to follow up on."

"Yeah?"

"Right before Newman shoots Andy he says, 'We don't want to do this.'"

"'We?'"

"Yeah, 'we.'"

**12**
———

J.P. SLOWLY CAME AWAKE in a different hospital room. His throat was raw. The shade was up and it was night; he could see the city lights. The only light in the room came from a fluorescent one that shown from beneath a cabinet, above the sink. The door to the room was closed almost all the way. A chair had been pulled up next to his bed and Tammy's light blue hoodie rested there, along with her Kindle. J.P. didn't know if it was 9 p.m. or the middle of the night.

He reached up and carefully felt the bandages on his head. The wound did not hurt, perhaps because it was still numb. He was groggy. He wondered if he would be allowed to go home the next day. He looked to see if there were any IVs in his arms; there were not. He assumed he was still feeling the after-affects of the pain meds and wondered if the wound would hurt once they wore off.

He was thirsty and would ask Tammy for water when she returned. He closed his eyes thinking maybe he could sleep more. But the shock and horror of the first gunshot rang out in his head from that morning, and he clearly recalled the overpowering sense of alarm that had gripped his chest. The smell of gunfire was still in his head. His heart rate increased as he vividly remembered trying to get out of the building, but being blocked in, running into Dowdy, and hearing the next blasts.

He opened his eyes and a tear shot down his cheek.

58

J.P. thought to himself that he would never forget the absolute terror that consumed him when he and Dowdy were hiding behind the turned-over conference room table in the darkness, and Gregory Newman rammed the door and screamed for Dowdy.

He wondered why Gregory hadn't shot at the lock on the door handle and barged in.

Maybe he didn't know for sure anyone was in there.

Maybe he didn't think he had time.

Perhaps God had steered him away.

J.P. remembered what Leena had said earlier about the lepers —and he closed his eyes and thanked God again for sparing his life.

Then he remembered something troubling Dowdy had said when they were hiding from Gregory. Right in the heat of it, Dowdy had whispered, "I should have killed the twerp when I had the chance."

*What was that all about?*

Dowdy had known it was Greg Newman.

J.P. thought of the families and loved ones of those who were killed that morning, grieving in their homes at that moment.

There were several light knocks at the door and it opened quietly. Bright light came from behind and silhouetted Tammy, who came in clutching several things against her chest.

"Hey, big guy," she whispered. "You awake?" She walked quietly to the bed, leaned in close, and kissed him. The lemony smell of her perfume comforted him.

"How do you feel?" she said.

"A little overwhelmed."

"Does it hurt?" She examined the new bandages.

"No. My throat's sore. What time is it?"

"Like 8:45. What's overwhelming you?" She gently touched his cheek. "Hmm?"

"I just can't believe that really went down."

"I bet. It's got to be surreal." She set two small containers of cranberry juice on the tray next to the bed, opened one, put a straw in, and held it up to his lips.

He drank. It tasted so good. He drank more.

"Easy. Take it slow."

He leaned back and tried to relax, wishing he was at his own place.

Tammy set his drink on the tray and rolled it closer so he could reach it. She pulled her chair closer to the bed and sat down.

"Greg was a nice guy," J.P. said. "The last person I'd think would ever do this. I mean, he was an awkward guy, but I never saw him lose his temper or threaten anyone. He seemed level-headed."

"We just don't know people. Think what must have been going on in his mind. He must've been tormented."

"I can't believe he shot those people . . . He told me he hadn't been himself lately."

"Really? I didn't know you knew him that well."

"I told you he confided in me about the Dowdy stuff. The debt."

"I know, but—"

"Then a couple weeks ago I saw him eating lunch alone in the break room and I sat down with my lunch. We talked. He hinted that his marriage wasn't great. I got the impression he was taking meds for something—depression or anxiety."

"I remember meeting his wife at that one Christmas party, the one at Juno's. She seemed nice."

"Yeah, she did. That's right, we talked in the food line. Jessica, I think it is. They seemed happy."

"They'd just bought a house, I remember that," Tammy said. "They had like three kids. Can you imagine what she's going through?"

"No. Not even close."

She rubbed his arm. "I think you're going to be able to go home tomorrow. I talked to the surgeon. Will you be up for that?"

"Oh, heck yeah. I'm ready now."

J.P. reached for the drink and took another sip, spilling it down his chin. They laughed.

It was quiet.

"How are *you*?" He squeezed her hand.

"Fine, compared to you. Mom and the sibs send their love. She wants to bring you a meal when you get home."

"Mmm. How about her sloppy joes?"

"I'll see what I can do."

"I've been thinking . . . I'm going to need to tell my dad about

Dowdy. The things Gregory told me—about the debt, the threats, and everything else."

"Everything?"

"I think so, yeah."

"Even the call I made to their house?" Tammy said.

"Yeah, honey."

Tammy took her hand away, dropped her head, and sighed.

It was silent for a moment and J.P. assumed they were both thinking the same thing.

"I know we probably have to say all that," Tammy said, "but Dowdy's going to be livid if he finds out we told the police about the domestic violence thing."

J.P. shrugged. "There's no way around it, Tam. The police are going to be looking for motive, why Gregory did this. We need to tell them everything we know—so they have all they need."

"I'm not suggesting we don't. I'm just . . . Dowdy scares me, J.P. He really scares me. The police filed a report that night I was there even though there were no charges. Isn't that enough?"

"Yeah, but if we don't mention it, they may never see that report. It's filed. It's old news. My dad needs to know, sweetie."

He reached out and took her hand.

Not much scared Tammy.

Dowdy's often volatile personality frightened him, too, but he wasn't about to say so.

"It'll be okay," J.P. said. "We'll talk to my dad. We'll tell him what we know. We'll tell him we're concerned about how Dowdy will respond. He'll know what to do from there. Like you always say, 'Jesus, take the wheel.'"

She chortled. "You got that right."

"You know what? I have to use the bathroom."

Tammy stood and backed her chair up. "Are you going to be able to walk?

"I'm fine." J.P. eased his way up to the edge of the bed and grunted as he set his bare feet on the cold floor. "Ah. Whew. Head-rush."

"Take it slow."

Tammy's phone vibrated. She went to check it while he headed slowly for the bathroom.

"Text from your mom," she said. "She wants to know if you're up to talking."

"Tonight?"

"Yes!"

"Definitely not!" He called out from the bathroom. "Tell her I'm fine but really tired. I'll see them tomorrow."

Tammy sat down and composed a text to Joanie.

When J.P. came back into the room, he said, "Where's my phone, babe?"

"You look really sexy in that gown."

"Very funny. If you like it that much maybe I'll take it home."

They laughed and he began to search for his phone.

"What do you need it for? Can't you just rest?" she said.

"I need to check email."

"Can't it wait till tomorrow?"

"I won't sleep. Come on, where is it?"

"It's in that closet sitting on top of your clothes with your wallet and watch."

He padded over, found the phone, crossed back to the bed, and gingerly climbed in. Tammy helped him get the pillows and covers situated.

"I'm gonna take off," she said. "I've got an early morning back at work."

"Thanks for coming, babe."

She gave him a quick hug and a kiss.

"Be careful going home," he said.

"Your mom's planning to come tomorrow. I think she wants to help get you settled back in at your place whenever they let you go."

"Is my car still at my office?"

"Yeah. Don't worry about that, okay? We'll get it tomorrow, sometime. I might be able to help at lunch or after work."

They kissed again and said goodnight.

When the door clicked closed, J.P. turned his phone on. The bright screen in the dark room showed a list of text messages. Three were from Christopher Dowdy. Each said the same thing: "Urgent. Call me. Urgent!"

**13**

—————

AFTER REVIEWING all of his texts and emails, and responding to a few important ones dealing with work, J.P. brushed his teeth and got in bed. He'd ignored the texts from Dowdy. The man had become known around the office for stirring up huge storms of controversy over what usually turned out to be minor issues. J.P. hoped this was one of those occasions. He certainly wasn't about to get on the phone with the man this late at night just after having had surgery.

But, in the back of his mind, J.P. worried he may lose sleep thinking about whatever it was Dowdy wanted.

There was a tap at the door and a nurse breezed in to check on J.P. Her name was Beverly and she efficiently examined his bandages, straightened his bed, and gave him fresh ice water and several extra-strength Tylenol. "Would you like the light over the sink turned off?"

J.P. said yes and thanked her.

When Beverly had gone, the room was dark and he finally closed his eyes and forced himself to relax. His head was starting to hurt slightly. He realized he should have texted Tammy to make sure she'd made it home okay, but he wasn't going to get up now. He carefully rolled onto one side, pulled the blankets up around his neck, and tried to clear his mind. The stark and horrific events of the morning replayed, but he eventually drifted off.

. . .

THE SHRILL RING of his phone across the black hospital room awoke J.P. with a jolt. He sat up on the edge of the bed in the black room, his head pounding and heart racing. The white glow from the phone pulsed with each ring. He had no clue what time it was. He got his bearings, slowly lowered himself to the cold floor, and walked toward the phone, not knowing the room, and not wanting to stub a toe.

He got to it and squinted at the bright screen.

The caller ID said it was Christopher Dowdy calling—2:39 a.m.

*This can't go on.*

"Hell-o?" J.P. answered with a nasty, questioning tone.

"J.P. It's about time—"

"Christopher, it's the middle of the night." His head throbbed. "What is it that couldn't possibly wait till tomorrow?"

"Did you get my texts?"

"Yeah, but I just had surgery, remember? I'm still in the hospital."

"If you'd have called me earlier, I wouldn't be calling now."

"Just . . . what is it, Chris? Make it quick."

"Okay, look, with what happened, with what Newman did, there are going to be a lot of questions. The media, the police—they're going to be all over this thing. I just want to make sure we're on the same page about everything—you and me."

"We? What are you even talking about right now?"

"Okay. I just need to find out from you what all you know, what Newman told you . . . about me?"

J.P.'s mind was blown. He was angry and frustrated. And he wondered what kind of bones Dowdy must have hiding in his closet. "Having to do with what?"

"Work. Debt. My dad's involvement. Etcetera."

"Chris, this isn't cool. My head is killing me. I was asleep, man. I'm not in a state to talk about this now."

"You should have called me when I texted you ten times," Dowdy blared. "The police are going to question us—"

"Stop making it sound like we're in on some big crime together.

This is ridiculous. I've done nothing wrong. I know you had or have gambling debts and—"

"And you know your girlfriend came to my place about a domestic dispute."

The direct confrontation blindsided J.P. Between the shooting, surgery, and lack of sleep, he was speechless.

"I'm *warning* you. I'm warning you not to tell the police about that or anything else Greg Newman may have told you about me."

The line went silent.

J.P. was flabbergasted. He was being threatened by this creep and he had no words.

"Get me? This is a warning," Dowdy said. "You only get one. Keep your mouth shut and all will be well—with you, with Tammy, with your whole police family."

J.P.'s face burned with rage.

But he needed to play this smartly.

He ran through a dozen responses in his mind.

"Chris, listen, do me a favor, let's talk about this tomorrow. I'm on pain meds. I'm groggy. My head's killing me. I'll be much clearer tomorrow."

"No, Deetz. This is *it*. You've been warned. Do what I say, or else."

The line went dead.

14

THE NEXT MORNING, Deetz and Brandon attended the 7 a.m. briefing at police headquarters and hit the streets. It was cool and gray outside with a light drizzle in the air, typical for Portland in May. They both wore their dark navy police jackets and ski caps.

"I want you to see that counselor Tidwell mentioned," Deetz said as Brandon drove them toward the hospital. They planned to visit Andy Grover and do a formal interview with J.P. about the shooting at his office building.

"Dad, no. Really. I don't need to. I'm fine," Brandon said.

"You may not realize it yet, but what we went through yesterday was traumatic, highly traumatic. Like, soul-shaking stuff."

"Believe me, I know."

"And, you shot a man—who died."

"Dad, please."

"Brandon, these things are about as heavy as you can get."

"I can handle it."

"Buddy, I've been doing this for thirty-five years. Can you just trust me on this?"

The car hummed along on the wet pavement.

"Have you found a church yet?" Deetz said.

"Not yet. I want to."

"What about a small group, like Christian guys you can confide in?"

"I'd like that, but I've been busy, Dad. Finishing school. The Academy. I've been going to classes and studying like every waking hour."

"I understand. And now you've got the pressure of starting a stressful new job."

"Yeah . . . I mean, it's a lot." Brandon's eyes suddenly got glassy.

"Let's do this," Deetz said. "How about if I call the counselor and see if she can fit you in at four o'clock one day this week. That way, you can be there four to five on company time and then clock off at five. Go home, be done. One and done."

Brandon shook his head and turned the Interceptor into the campus of the hospital.

"Just walk through what happened with her," Deetz said. "She'll ask some questions about it, about how you feel about it, and that'll be it. And then, if you like her, you'll have her as a contact from here on out, whenever you need to vent."

Brandon glanced at Deetz. "I really don't want to, Dad."

"Tidwell's going to ask you, I guarantee it."

Brandon sighed.

"Trust me on this, Brandon. Please. It's one hour of your life."

He swung the police vehicle into a space and put it in park.

"I have her card," Brandon said. "I'll call her."

"That's what I'm talking about."


PORTLAND POLICE OFFICER Andy Grover was due to be discharged from the hospital later that day and was chomping at the bit to get home. He was sitting up in his hospital bed on the fifth floor when Deetz and Brandon arrived to see him.

Deetz had gotten to know Andy briefly over the past ten years or so. He introduced him to Brandon. Andy was probably in his early forties. He was a wide, stocky guy, balding with brown hair on the sides and a bushy brown mustache. He was wearing a hospital gown in bed and Deetz couldn't tell where he'd been shot. He couldn't seem to sit still.

"You can't get a decent cup of coffee in here," Andy said with a New Jersey accent. "Look at it. It's the color of weak tea, I swear."

Deetz and Brandon stood, one on each side of the bed.

"Here, move this tray out of the way." Andy grunted as he shoved the tray toward Brandon, who wheeled it over against the wall. All of the thick brown plastic plates and bowls on the tray were empty, so it looked as if Andy liked the food much better than the coffee.

"Oh, hand me my glasses off that tray, would ya?"

Brandon got Andy his black eyeglasses as Deetz explained to him that Tidwell had asked them to handle the investigation of the shooting.

"Tell us how it went down, from your perspective?" Deetz said, as he got out his pad and pen.

"I was wrapping up my shift that morning, kind of cruising in and out of Gilmore Commons on my way back to headquarters. They've had a lot of homeless people around there and we're supposed to try to keep it clear." Andy used exaggerated hand motions as he spoke. "Anyway, when I came down Hawthorne I noticed a white subcompact parked on the plaza at the office complex where it happened—I forget the name of it."

"Farris-Junger," Deetz said.

"Correct. So the car was where it shouldn't be. There's no parking where it was. So I drove in there and stopped like forty yards from it and I see a guy in the driver's seat. I thought he may be sleeping, or that it may be a delivery guy. So I got out and approached the car on foot."

"Had you gotten the plates yet?"

"No, I was going to do that when I got closer. So, as I'm walking over, the guy gets out really quickly and yells something like, 'Please, go. Please, just get out of here.' He's waving me away."

"Okay," Deetz said.

"So, I hold up my hands and continue walking toward him, slowly, but his car is between us. He's shielded by it while I'm out in the open. Then he bends into the car, pops up again, and yells, 'You need to leave now officer.' And right then a woman shows up and I'm like, 'Oh, crap.' I'm telling him to come out from behind the car. I can't see his hands. It got dicey."

"Was your gun drawn at this point?"

"Once the lady appeared, I drew my weapon."

"How far away from him were you at that point?" Deetz said.

"Twenty yards or so. And I can see the look on his face. When he saw the lady, he freaked. He called her name. He knew her. I turned to tell her to run and I heard him scream, 'We don't want to do this.' And, bam, I'm hit."

"He said, 'we?'" Deetz said.

Andy pursed his lips and nodded. "The guy was not playing with a full deck."

"Where did he get you?" Deetz said.

Andy pushed the blankets down and yanked his gown up, revealing huge bandages around the top of his right thigh, surrounded by black and blue skin. "When I hit the ground my gun bounced away. He was around his car fast. His eyes were just black, and huge. He picked up my gun and threw it away on his way to the woman. I tried to get over to help her, but I just couldn't stand. I'm lucky he didn't shoot me again."

"Then what?"

"I heard him say her name, Jackie. I couldn't make out the rest, but his tone was almost apologetic. Like he'd been with me. Like he didn't want to do it. Like he was sorry." Andy shook his head. "Thank God she lived. I'm actually surprised."

"Then what?"

"Danny showed up." Andy shook his head and his eyes flooded with tears. He covered them with a doughy hand and his chest lurched several times as he tried to hold back the emotions. "He called it in, thank God, because I would have bled out. The lady, too, probably. The shooter blasted the door and went in the building. Paramedics got there fast; they'd been right around the corner getting coffee. But, Danny, man..." Tears shot down Andy's face. "He went right in after the guy. Brave as hell." Andy cried softly, knowing Danny had died once inside the building. "Sorry, boys."

15

———

BRANDON SUGGESTED they take the steps down to J.P.'s room on the fourth floor. Deetz agreed and as they headed down in the stairwell Brandon voiced what was weighing on his heart after speaking with officer Andy Grover.

"I can't get my head around these kinds of shootings," he said. "People are deranged. This Newman guy knew he had problems, why didn't he check himself in somewhere—or just shoot himself?"

A cute, brunette nurse wearing light green scrubs passed them as she jogged up the steps. She and Brandon made eye contact, smiled, and said 'hey.'

"He probably thought seeing all those doctors and getting the right meds would make everything okay," Deetz said. "I mean, if it were me, that's what I'd be hoping, wouldn't you? No one wants to put themselves in a mental facility, or admit they need to be there."

They got to the fourth floor, opened the door, looked for signs, and headed toward J.P.'s room.

"Think about the people from the Bible who had demons," Deetz said.

"Whoa. That came out of left field." Brandon looked at him oddly. "What do you mean?"

"I don't think that's ever changed. I think people still have demons. Of course, no one talks about it."

"Dad, come on. For real?"

"Think about it. What's changed to make it any different now than it was then?" Deetz said. "People had demons, evil spirits. It was common. Jesus rebuked them and drove them out; sometimes his disciples did."

"So, you think Gregory Newman had a demon?" Brandon stopped outside J.P.'s door, genuinely curious.

Deetz shrugged. "Some people had more than one. Mary Magdalene had seven."

"Dad," Brandon chuckled and looked around. "No one thinks like you do."

Deetz squared up with Brandon and spoke quietly. "I'm just saying, think of the sheer evil it took to do what Greg Newman did. J.P. insists he was a nice, mild-mannered guy. Something got into him, something evil that overcame him and took over."

Brandon stared at his dad, wide-eyed.

"I've thought about this a lot since becoming a Christian, Brandon, dealing with crooks and criminals," Deetz said. "I've just never told anyone but you. It's just something I wonder about and think about."

For the past three or four years, Brandon's dad arose before sunrise and read his Bible in the quiet house or on the screened porch with a mug of steaming coffee next to him.

*Every morning.*

He knew that Book.

It had become his anchor. His armor. And compass.

It was where he left his worries and girded himself with strength each day.

Even though Deetz and Joanie weren't strong believers when the kids were little, Brandon remembered they would always lie around with Dad at night and talk before bed.

One thing Brandon remembered most about his childhood—more than anything else—was that his dad would ask each of the kids how their day had been, what was fun about it, what had been difficult? He would listen to whatever they had to say. He would be in no hurry. And the kids would lie around in their jammies and talk, ramble even. It was like therapy for each of them.

That act alone said more to Brandon about his dad's character than anything he could have ever taught them about the Bible. And now that his dad was a Christian, he had become even more compassionate and understanding.

Brandon had meant to find a church or small group; those hadn't been just words to placate his dad. He wanted that foundation that he now saw burning bright in his dad and mom. He'd just been so busy with college and police studies that he'd put it on a back burner.

His dad's notions about demons piqued his curiosity.

"Where is that in the Bible?" Brandon said.

Deetz, who was about to knock on J.P.'s door, stopped and looked at him. "Matthew, Mark, Luke. Check it out. Ephesians talks about putting on the armor of God so we can defend ourselves against the schemes of the enemy. Being a cop, that's especially good."

Brandon chuckled at his dad—and took note.


WHEN BRANDON and Deetz entered J.P.'s hospital room they found him sitting up in bed eating breakfast on the tray in front of him.

"The boys in blue," J.P. said, with a mouthful of pancakes.

"That doesn't look half bad," Brandon said, taking a piece of bacon off J.P.'s plate.

"Give it back! I'm recovering."

Brandon laughed, took a bite, and tossed the remainder back on the plate.

"I don't want that now!"

Brandon took it back and dropped it in his mouth.

As they pulled up chairs on each side of the bed, Deetz asked how J.P. was doing and explained that they needed to ask some questions about the morning of the shooting, and the people involved.

After J.P. had walked them through his movements that morning up to the point when he got shot, Deetz turned the questioning to J.P.'s knowledge about what was going on at work between Gregory Newman and Christopher Dowdy.

"Everything started turning bad when Dowdy fired Jarod Jenkins and took over running the company," J.P. said. "Right away, Dowdy and Gregory butted heads. Greg did everything by the book and watched the company spending like a hawk. Dowdy didn't want that. He wanted a yes man. He wanted Greg to pay the bills without asking questions."

"How do you know all this?" Brandon said.

"Greg and I were friends, sort of. He confided in me. He said his wife wanted him to tell someone higher up in the company what was going on."

"She told us Dowdy had gambling debts," Deetz said.

J.P. nodded. "Greg showed me a text he got instructing him—it was a threat, really—to withdraw company money to pay off some big debt. He thought the Mob had gotten involved and were coming after him and the company to pay Dowdy's gambling debt."

"How much money?" Deetz said.

"That was a hundred grand, Greg said."

"Where or how or to whom did they want Greg to pay the money?"

"An offshore account. Online. It was supposed to be completely secure. Private."

"Did he do it?" Brandon said.

"They gave him a deadline," J.P. said somberly. "Yesterday. The day he lost it."

"Shift gears," Deetz said. "The affair Dowdy had with Greg's wife. She claims he did it just to spite Greg. Who knows, maybe even to get him to quit. What do you know about all that?"

J.P. shook his head and rolled the tray away. "The affair ruined Greg's life. He told me he wasn't coping. He was having anxiety attacks. Depressed. I invited him to church, but he never came. He'd lost all trust in Jessica. I mean, that destroyed him. Dowdy did that."

Brandon and Deetz looked at each other and locked eyes momentarily. Brandon was thinking back to their conversation about demons and wondered if his dad was thinking the same thing.

"Dowdy is a womanizer and everyone knows it," J.P. said. "He's got the worst reputation . . . He called me in the middle of the night last night and threatened me not to talk to you about him."

"You're kidding me right now," Brandon said.

"Huh-uh," J.P. said. "You asked what was wrong with Tammy yesterday?" He sighed and paused. "She was on-call last winter and had to go out to a domestic disturbance late one night at a high-rise in the city. It was Dowdy. His wife had called nine-one-one. Tammy met the police out there. Darlene, his wife, had bruises on her neck and arms."

"For real?" Brandon said.

J.P. nodded. "Dowdy reeked of alcohol. The sliding glass door leading to the balcony was cracked. The place was a mess, furniture was broken, as if there'd been a big fight."

"Did they arrest him?" Deetz said.

J.P. stared at Deetz. "Nope. Darlene denied everything when Tammy got there. She said she fell down the steps of the loft. Tammy talked to her in private while the police were still there. Tammy believed she was lying. Darlene was crying and trembling uncontrollably. Tammy thinks she was in fear for her life, but she wouldn't tell because she was so afraid of Dowdy. When Tammy got home, she was really shaken up. She was seriously worried about Darlene."

Brandon was furious. "I could tell that guy was a jerk from the second he walked into your room yesterday. That guy needs a smackdown."

"So, no charges that night?" Deetz said.

"No. They filed a report but no charges. And that's not all. After the police left, he came onto Tammy."

"What do you mean?" Brandon blurted.

"When she was leaving, he stepped into the hallway and said something like, 'J.P. has good taste.'"

Deetz's head dropped.

Brandon fumed.

"He made a reference to liking black women," J.P. said.

"Dude!" Brandon stood in a fit.

"Tammy said in all the experiences she's ever had with domestic disputes, she's never had the feeling she got that night. Like, warning signs blaring. That's why she acted like she did when he came in my room yesterday. There's a history there. And you saw how he acted. And I'm not even sure she told me everything about that night. More may've happened that she doesn't want to tell me. He gives her the creeps, big time."

"No wonder Greg Newman was after the guy!" Brandon said.

"Don't say that, son." Deetz shook his head slowly. "When things get emotional it's our job to keep calm. We don't share our opinion. And we especially don't embrace the actions of cold-blooded killers."

"There's rumors he's had affairs with some of the women at work," J.P. said. "I have no idea if they're true or not."

"Do you know who?" Deetz said.

"One was Carrie Sandowski—the woman who died," J.P. said blankly.

"No way," Brandon said.

"I don't know if it's true—that they had an affair. It's just a rumor. Like I said, she was engaged recently."

"Any others?" Deetz said.

"I don't know any more names," J.P. said.

"What about Dowdy's dad? Greg's wife told us he got involved with the company," Deetz said.

"Consultant. That's all anybody knows. He's a 'consultant' for the company," J.P. said.

"Paid?" Deetz said.

"Oh, yeah," J.P. said. "Greg said he paid one invoice to the guy for fifteen grand."

"I smell a rat," Brandon said.

Again, his dad looked at him as if he should keep his opinions to himself.

Deetz finished taking notes and the conversation turned to J.P.'s injury and when he would return home and back to work. J.P. was hoping to be released later that day, and Deetz assured him Joanie would be there to help get him checked out and situated back at his apartment.

Deetz and Brandon said their goodbyes and headed for the door. Deetz warned J.P. that he may have post-traumatic stress disorder and encouraged him to talk to a counselor if he got overwhelmed.

"Hold up," J.P. called as they headed for the door. "I forgot something."

They came back and stood at the foot of J.P.'s bed.

"When Dowdy and I were hiding in the conference room he said something like, "I should've killed that twerp when I had the chance.' About Greg Newman. That hit me as weird, like they'd had some kind of confrontation."

**16**

———

By 3:30 P.M., Deetz was wiped out and looking forward to the end of the shift. He and Brandon had been called on to respond to two different car accidents in the city, a smash-and-grab at a beauty supply store, and the report of a stolen car from an auto repair shop. Once again, Brandon had been overwhelmed and somewhat frustrated by the amount of paperwork they had to complete.

"I made that appointment—with the shrink," Brandon said while driving the Interceptor just outside city limits. "She fit me in today, so I need to head that way soon."

"For what time?" Deetz looked at his watch.

"Four."

"Well, shoot, we better get you back to your car. Head that way." Deetz was often stunned how Brandon waited until the last minute to speak up about things. But he was glad he'd taken the initiative to make the appointment. *Probably out of a fear of Tidwell.*

Brandon put on his blinker and eased the SUV into a turn lane to head back to the station.

"What will you do the rest of the shift?" Brandon said.

"Well, I had a lot more planned for us today on the investigation, but that all got sidetracked. I may try to fit in an interview on the way home."

"With who?"

Deetz got a text and looked at his phone. It was from Joanie:

"J.P. getting released. Doing paperwork now. Hope to get him back to his place soon. Leena's at work. How are you guys?"

He told Brandon that his brother was being released and texted Joanie back with an update.

"What'd you just ask me?" Deetz said.

"Who you'll interview?"

"Oh, I'm hoping J.P.'s former boss or the lady who got shot on the plaza, Jackie Brooks. She's home already. They both live in the city. I need to find out if either can talk now."

"I hate to miss it."

"I'll fill you in on all the gory details."


WITHIN TWENTY MINUTES, Deetz was seated at a high-top table at a dark tavern named Brandy's in downtown Portland, which Jarod Jenkins said was right around the corner from his residence. Deetz got a cup of coffee from the bar, sat at a sticky table by the window, and reviewed his notes.

He thought about Gregory Newman and Christopher Dowdy and the darkness of it all as he looked out at the city streets, which were now lined with ugly, neon orange barrels—Mayor Barbara Meeks' brilliant idea to prevent drive-by shootings.

The mayor's novel idea to defund the police had resulted in a twenty-seven-million-dollar budget cut and a record number of homicides in 2021. The budget cuts had led to an acute staffing shortage. Sergeant Tidwell had told the media the Police Bureau was "running on fumes," and would require 840 officer hires over the next five years to keep Portland safe. The mayor's response? She ordered Portland Police to suspend minor traffic stops so officers could focus on "more immediate threats."

*More brilliance.*

Deetz was super relieved to be in his last year. Although he and Joanie would never be "empty nesters"—because of Leena's special needs—they looked forward to exploring other cities as possible retirement destinations.

But he did fear for Brandon's future as a cop. Portland had become Oregon's largest city, and deadly violence was increasing at a faster rate than nearly every major metropolis in the U.S. Thanks to the volatile political climate, the city was overrun with gangs, violent protests, fights, and retaliation killings.

Deetz hated to think of himself as a grouchy old man, but he'd come to the point where he simply didn't trust politicians. And he was infuriated by the lawlessness that was becoming the new normal in his city.

The latest craze was the brazen smash-and-grab robberies like Brandon and he had responded to that morning, where large groups of thugs met on social media and agreed to rob the same store at the same exact time. They all showed up at once, coming from all directions in their own vehicles, and simply took over the store, smashing glass showcases and leaving with whatever they wanted. It was dangerous and terrifying for patrons who happened to be in the store at the time of the events.

Bells rang as the door to Brandy's opened and a tall, thin man with curly blonde hair spotted Deetz, approached, and introduced himself as Jarod Jenkins. Deetz stood, they shook hands, and Jenkins commented how much Deetz and J.P. looked alike.

Jenkins got a bottle of Perrier from the bar. They sat across from each other and made small talk for several minutes. Jenkins was a business grad from Harvard, a long-distance runner, book lover, and history buff. He lived alone in a nearby apartment and seemed quiet, thoughtful, and intelligent. He said, even with all the trouble the city of Portland was going through, he couldn't think of any place he'd rather live.

Deetz could think of a lot of places.

Jenkins had initially heard about the shooting at Jumpy Jim's on Twitter, then got more details from several former co-worker friends who still worked there. He said he'd texted J.P. and was relieved he was going to be okay.

"J.P. told me he loved it when you headed up the company," Deetz said. "Can you go through with me how Christopher Dowdy came to be more involved and why you eventually left? And we'll get into Gregory Newman as we go . . ."

With his hands on his waist, Jenkins inhaled deeply and leaned his head and shoulders way back. Still looking at the ceiling, he exhaled through a small o-shaped mouth. His shoulders slumped and he looked at Deetz.

"Dowdy was never supposed to have a part in operations. That was never in the blueprints. If it had been, I never would have taken the job in the first place," Jenkins said. "He was an investor, and I have a hunch his dad was probably behind that. The other main investor, Will Tomason, was involved, mainly in the early planning stages. Will hired me. He also hired Greg Newman—and J.P. Everything was going smoothly. The first few years were solid. And we had a good plan in place for the future. But it all hit the fan when Dowdy got involved."

"Why did he get involved?" Deetz questioned.

"His words: 'There are a hundred ways we can be making higher profits.' He was adamant that we start doing so." Jenkins shook his head as if shaking off a bad dream. "I don't know how much J.P. told you, but from day one we were a green company. Eco-friendly. Socially-minded. We worked only with independent, family-owned coffee farmers. And we used nothing but the best beans, from premium arabica coffee plants.

"So one day in February, Dowdy shows up at our offices, which was weird. He never did that. He was never involved before that. We never saw him," Jenkins continued. "He demanded an office, a computer, phone, expense account, the works. I was forced to give him an existing office, which belonged to Gregory Newman."

"Oh no," Deetz said.

Jenkins frowned and nodded. "Greg got moved from a nice office with windows and a big desk to a tiny cubicle in the maze. And Dowdy rode him like a wild horse and put him away wet. He was all over Greg to slash budgets, cut costs, postpone employee raises. It was . . . how can I describe it? Irrational. He was telling Greg to pay the bills without asking any questions and Greg wasn't used to that. He'd been a bigger player than that, because I'd relied on him to sniff out any problems. He wanted to be involved with the decision-making. The whole thing just got so messy, so fast. I think he wanted to force Greg out. I didn't like what was happening, what Dowdy was doing."

"What else was he doing?" Deetz said.

"Dowdy brought in his dad as a consultant. We were paying him like two-hundred-fifty dollars an hour—"

"Alexander Dowdy?"

"Correct. He was on the clock for twenty to thirty hours a week. That's a chunk of change for us. Up till then, Greg had us running lean and mean, so that was a huge added expense. But the biggest thing was when the Dowdys hired an expensive logistics company I'd never heard of to come in and redo our whole distribution process." He paused and took a long drink from the green bottle of Perrier. "That was the last straw."

"What was it called?"

"Laser Direct. It was a nightmare. Everything was late. We were late getting our beans back to the States, late packaging, late on orders, and late getting product into stores. I went into Chris's office one night we were both working late and I said, 'If we don't go back to the way we were doing it, I'm gone.' He looked up at me and said, 'Then you're gone. Let's make this your last day.'"

"Whoa." Deetz wrote down the name of the company and reviewed his notes. "So he came in to cut costs, but it sounds like costs went up with his dad involved."

"Way up. And operations suffered, dramatically."

"Tell me about Gregory Newman and what you think may've led him to commit such an atrocious attack?"

Jenkins put both hands flat on the table and looked down for a long time. His fingers were long and bony. Finally, he looked up at Deetz. "Greg was odd. He was somewhat awkward. He was quite shy, really. But he was amazing at his job. He was smart. I mean, he could follow a money trail like a bloodhound. That's why Will hired him. I could ask him anything about expenses or cashflow, and he would know the answer or find it really fast. Up until Dowdy came in, Greg seemed fine. I mean, like I said, he was always a bit awkward to talk to, but we all accepted that and embraced him. He told me once how much he loved his job and our work. But he and Dowdy butted heads, literally from day one. I think he was too smart for Dowdy."

"Do you know if they had a confrontation at any time?" Deetz said.

"They argued a few times—in meetings." Jenkins' mouth turned down and he shook his head with a look of frustration. "Dowdy tried to make a fool of him a couple times, but he did that to almost everyone. It wasn't just Greg. That's all I can remember."

"How did the affair between Dowdy and Greg's wife impact Greg and things at work?"

Jenkins shrugged. "I don't know much about that. It's all just a sorry mess. I heard Greg got fired last week. The fact is, Dowdy couldn't keep him around if he wanted to do whatever he was trying to do with company funds. Greg was just too smart."

"Yeah, Dowdy fired Greg last Friday," Deetz said. "Do you know—"

"Actually, it was the old man who fired Greg," Jenkins said.

Deetz did a doubletake. "Are you sure about that?"

"Yes. I'm still close with a few people over there. The guy who worked alongside Greg told me."

"What's his name?"

Jenkins hesitated. "Kyle Ford."

Deetz jotted it down.

"Can you tell me about other affairs Dowdy may've been having?"

Jenkins turned away for a moment. "I don't really think that's for me to say."

"Did you know Greg had guns? Did you know of any threat or any warning that something like this may happen?"

Jenkins shook his head. "Didn't know he was a gun owner. No warnings."

"Why else do you think Greg may have been fired or on bad terms with Dowdy and his dad?"

"Look, it's a known fact Christopher's a gambler. And he has, or had, a large amount of debt." Jenkins leaned over the table closer to Deetz and lowered his voice. "Let me ask you something. Is any of this going to get back to Dowdy? What I say to you here, right now? Is he going to know I said it?"

"Not now. If it ever gets to the courts, that could change."

"Here's the thing. Greg Newman thought Laser Direct may have been a shadow company Dowdy and his dad created to siphon funds from the company—to pay for Chris's gambling debts, or line their pockets, or whatever. I thought it sounded far-fetched, but now I wonder."

"Were you aware Greg Newman received a threat to pay money —with Jumpy Jim funds—into an offshore account? This was supposedly an organized crime group who chose this way to collect on Christopher Dowdy's gambling debt?"

Jenkins looked at his watch. "I've got to get going soon. But . . . that happened after I was gone. I heard about it—through the grapevine."

"I guess the day the shooting occurred was the day of the deadline—for Greg to pay the money . . ."

Jenkins stood up, looked around the mostly empty bar, and finally leveled his gaze at Deetz. "That wasn't the Mob," he whispered and pointed a finger at Deetz. "That was the *Dowdys*." He turned around, upset, and took several steps toward the door. "What Greg did was unforgiveable. An atrocity, like you said. But there's more to it. It sounds like you're on the right track. Where there's smoke, there's fire."

Jenkins walked across the dark room. "Tell J.P. I said hi." He opened the door, stopped, and looked at Deetz intently. "Be careful."

**17**

———————

After his better-than-expected counseling session with the beautiful psychologist, Dr. Terri Wallender, Brandon got back to his apartment by 5:35 Tuesday evening. As usual, the first thing he did was head for his bedroom to get out of the uniform and put on some sweats and flipflops.

He went out to the kitchen, which smelled strongly of foreign food. Smooth jazz played from a Bluetooth speaker.

"Hey, what up?" said Clarence, his roommate, who was heating something in the microwave.

"What *is* that?" Brandon called over the music. "It smells like something from . . . Istanbul."

Clarence laughed heartily and turned the music down. "That, my rookie friend, is corn fritters and tofu, served with a Thai sweet chili sauce. Vegetarian. Gluten-free."

"Of course."

Brandon had met Clarence the first day of police training. They'd quickly become friends and decided to room together to save on rent. Their two-bedroom apartment was located on the outskirts of downtown Portland. It was situated on the fourth floor of a popular apartment complex and had a fair-sized living room, a swimming pool, and a workout facility on the premises.

Clarence retrieved his fragrant dinner with huge white oven mitts the size of firefighter gear and plopped down at the kitchen table, which looked like toy furniture compared to his strapping frame. At age twenty-six, Clarence Waters stood six-feet, three-inches tall and weighed two-hundred-twenty pounds. An African American with large, bright eyes and a one-inch afro, there wasn't an ounce of fat on him. His nickname at police training had been "Stone," and he proudly touted a body mass index of 22.5.

"How'd it go with that shrink?" Clarence said, blowing on a steaming spoonful of his entrée.

"Oh man, dude, she was a knockout." Brandon chose one of his many frozen pizzas from the freezer and turned on the oven without looking at the instructions on the box because he knew them by heart.

"Well, that's what matters, I guess," Clarence jested, "since the counseling is only for PTSD."

"No, she was really good," Brandon said. "I give my old man credit. She asked great questions and just let me ramble. I really didn't think I needed to talk to anyone, but the way she did it—stuff came out that was good. It felt really good."

"Like what?"

"Dude, these sessions are confidential. I can't divulge anything —other than the fact that *Doctor Wallender* was about the most gorgeous middle-aged woman I've ever laid eyes on. I think she was falling for me a little bit."

They laughed. But the truth was, Brandon hadn't slept well the night of the shooting. The session gave him the chance to tell the doctor he'd tossed and turned most of the night, reliving every second of the day's profound events. Dr. Wallender said the lack of sleep was normal after such an ordeal.

"How was your day?" Brandon said. "Catch any bad guys?"

"Eh," Clarence said with a mouthful. "Rickert gets on my last nerve, but we're good, I guess."

Harold Rickert was the senior officer who was mentoring Clarence during his field training. Deetz had warned Clarence that Rickert was as "old school" as they came.

"We went to a liquor store that had been held up, over on East Howard Street."

"Ew, wrong side of the tracks."

"You got that right. Perp wore a full mask and gloves. Had a sawed-off shotgun. Owner shows us the video from the security cam. Right off the bat, Rickert says the perp's black. I said, 'What? We can't see any skin. Guy could've been white, Asian, Hispanic. Rickert goes, 'Only blacks wear their pants that low.' And he said the type of shotgun he had was typical for black gang members."

This wasn't the first time Clarence had intimated that Rickert was racist. Brandon had asked Deetz about it in private and Deetz had said Rickert was old-fashioned, tough-as-nails, and could indeed be racist, but he'd never worked directly with him. Rickert had also lost his wife to cancer a year earlier.

"How does he treat you?" Brandon said.

"Okay. I guess. But those type of things bother me, man. I'm sure he must know it." Clarence swept his spoon around in the plastic entrée container, took the last bite, and went to the kitchen. "He's set in his ways for sure. I feel like he has to try really hard to treat me like a partner. He came right out and told me today he doesn't like doing field training with rookies."

"You're kidding."

"No." Clarence continued cleaning up in the kitchen. "Rickert said he's told them repeatedly he doesn't want to do it, but they're all required to take turns doing it."

"He must not have a lot of time left." Brandon said as he put his pizza in the oven, grabbed a Diet Coke out of the fridge and got a plate and napkins. "My dad's in his early-sixties and he retires later this year. Once you put in thirty-five you get full pension."

"Rickert looks ten years older than your dad. He should be long gone by now."

They laughed and Clarence turned off his music and grabbed a large gym bag from a chair in the living room. "I'm out, man."

"What is it tonight?" Brandon said, knowing Clarence worked out at one venue or another almost every night.

"You ain't gonna believe it. Yoga class!"

"What?" Brandon screeched. "It's got to be a girl."

Clarence's face lit up with a huge, gleaming smile. "What can I say? When your hygienist invites you to work-out, you say 'yes.' I don't care what it is!"

. . .

BRANDON ATE all but one slice of the meat-lovers' pizza while switching channels back and forth between the Seattle Mariners' game and CNN. It'd only been a day-and-a-half since the shooting at J.P.'s office and it had already been replaced in the headlines by another shooting at a warehouse in Dallas.

Brandon got up from the couch and went to his bedroom to try to find his Bible. He wanted to read more about the topic of demons. He found it on the top shelf in his closet, tossed it on the couch, and cleaned up his dinner dishes.

A text came in from his dad wanting to know how the counseling went and stating that he'd had an interesting interview that afternoon with J.P.'s former boss, Jarod Jenkins. The case mystified Brandon. He finished in the kitchen and called his dad.

"Your mom got your brother situated back at his place today," Deetz said.

"Yeah, he told me. I called him to see how he was. He sounded good; a little grumpy," Brandon said. "Do you need someone to go with you to get his car?"

"Nope. Mom and Tammy went just a little while ago. Thanks, though."

Brandon told his dad about the counseling session, and Deetz admitted he too had had a difficult time sleeping the night of the shooting. Brandon left out the part about how gorgeous Dr. Wallender was.

Brandon inquired about the interview with Jarod Jenkins, and Deetz told him how Dowdy showed up at Jumpy Jim's suddenly in February and Jenkins was forced to give him Gregory Newman's office. He also explained how Dowdy rode Newman hard, got his dad involved in the business, and hired Laser Direct to oversee distribution—which was a complete fail. And about how Jenkins got fired on the spot. And that it was Dowdy's dad who actually fired Newman.

Enthralled by all the details, Brandon found himself pacing back and forth on the balcony. He could see his breath in the cold, dark night air, and a thousand stars lit up the sky.

"Jenkins thinks the Dowdys may have made up Laser Direct just to siphon money from Jumpy Jim's," Deetz said. "He also implied that the threat Greg Newman got from the Mob didn't really come from the Mob, but from the Dowdys."

"What?" Brandon stopped cold. "So Dowdy threatened Newman like using a burner phone or something? It makes sense! That way, Dowdy gets company funds into an offshore account, and he can pay his debts off with it."

Brandon was appalled that someone could stoop so low. At the same time, he couldn't fathom why Greg Newman didn't tell the other owner, or the board of directors, or call the police—anything but do what he did.

Although the shooting and motives and mysteries behind it were reprehensible, Brandon found himself completely fascinated by the case. Now he knew why his dad did what he'd done for thirty-five years. It was a job like no other.

"I set up an interview with Christopher Dowdy for tomorrow," Deetz said.

"For real?" Brandon said, excitedly.

"He wanted his dad there and I said no. We'll talk to the dad separately."

"What time? Where?"

"For some reason he insisted we do it at Eastbank Esplanade. Eleven a.m." Eastbank Esplanade was a city park right on the Willamette River. "I'm going to work up questions tonight or tomorrow morning. If you think of things to ask, jot them down and we'll compare notes before we meet him."

"Dad, what do we do if we catch him in a lie or if he admits to some of this stuff?"

"We arrest him," Deetz said flatly. "There's something about this guy . . . he seems like the type who would sell his mother's soul to save himself."

"Man, this is intense."

"It is. You're conducting an investigation usually only seasoned police get to work."

"I think it's in my blood, Dad."

"I think so, too, Brandon."

**18**

———————

BRANDON HAD BEEN sound asleep for three hours when he awoke suddenly and shot straight up in bed. It was pitch black in his room except for the red numbers on his bedside clock, which read 2:09 a.m. He sat still, listening intently for something that may have awoken him, but heard only silence.

Wearing no shirt and checkered boxers, he got out of bed, crossed to the window, and looked through the slats to the quiet street below. Other than a guy bundled up walking his little dog, there was no movement. He stared at the man and his dog, wide-eyed.

He never usually had trouble sleeping soundly through the night. He hadn't been dreaming or thinking about the shooting; at least, he didn't remember doing so.

Brandon knew Clarence was in his room because he'd heard him come in just before he'd drifted off to sleep.

Brandon stood there wide awake, as if he'd slept eight hours. That was not good, because he needed to be up at 5:45 a.m. He thought of J.P. back home at his apartment and wondered if he was able to sleep with the bandages on his head. He wondered if Tammy ever slept over there, but didn't think they did that. Tammy was quite a fervent Christian and had been a good influence on J.P. in that department. Brandon stewed for a moment about not having a girlfriend and got a bit anxious because he was finished with college now and that's where you were supposed to meet your spouse, according to many.

He padded into the bathroom on the cold floor thinking if he went to church or joined a small group like his dad suggested, maybe he would meet someone there. He made his way through the living room where moonlight cast long shadows into the apartment. In the kitchen he got a drink of water from a cold gallon jug in the fridge and stood there in the dark listening to the hum of the refrigerator.

Dr. Wallender had told him that difficulty sleeping and staying asleep were symptoms of PTSD, as well as feeling on edge or on guard, as if danger was lurking around every corner. He didn't necessarily feel that way. He was just simply hyper alert.

The water had given him a chill, so he went to his room, put on flip-flops, and threw a hoodie on, then walked back out to the living room. He opened the sliding glass doors and walked out onto the balcony, which was so small it could only fit two chairs and Clarence's tiny hibachi.

It was a crisp May night and the moon was bright. He got a whiff of cigarette smoke and looked through the black railing to the street below where the dog-walker was seated on a bench, puffing away. Brandon wondered why the guy was up so late and thought perhaps he may've just gotten home from a late shift at work, or his wife and he were having a fight, or he just couldn't sleep.

It was cold and Brandon realized the night air would just keep him up, so he went back inside and slid the door closed. He noticed his Bible on the couch in the moonlight. He went over, picked it up, dropped onto the couch, and turned on the small lamp on the end table.

He thought about what his dad had said, flipped to the topical index in back, and looked up 'demons,' but found 'devil' first. The verses listed compared the devil to a 'wolf,' a 'roaring lion,' and a 'serpent.'

His mom and dad had always attempted to instill solid moral values in the kids. And within the past three to four years, they'd all started going to church, kind of following the lead of J.P. and Tammy. Since then, Brandon had noticed that his parents had really begun to live out their faith. It showed in their relationship, in their fun-loving spirit toward Leena, and in their steadfast faith about Deetz's job and their future.

While both J.P. and Leena had been baptized, Brandon had not. It wasn't because he didn't consider himself a Christian, he did, it was more because the opportunity had never presented itself and he hadn't pursued it. It was the same with Christianity in general. In the back of his mind he believed in God, but it was not something he had engaged in as much as he probably should.

Under 'character of the devil,' the index listed scriptures stating that the devil was 'presumptuous' . . . 'proud' . . . 'powerful' . . . 'wicked' . . . 'subtle' . . . 'deceitful' . . . 'fierce and cruel.' Brandon sat there in the quiet and re-read each word.

He then found a category beneath 'devil' entitled 'the wicked.' It listed scriptures stating the wicked were 'children of the devil' . . . 'possessed by the devil' . . . 'blinded by the devil' . . . as well as 'deceived' . . . 'ensnared' . . . and 'troubled by the devil.'

As he turned the pages to find one of the references in Luke, his heart broke for Gregory Newman's wife, Jessica. She was now forced to live with the dark aftermath of what her deeply disturbed husband had done. She would have to move away. If she didn't, how would she cope with the reaction of people who learned she was the widow of the monster who shot up the coffee company offices in Portland?

Brandon found Luke four and closed his eyes. He clearly remembered the exact, sickening look on Greg Newman's face when Deetz shined his flashlight on him in that black hallway—it was an empty, pasty look of deadness. An uncaring, expressionless ghost of a face that cried out, 'Shoot me. I'm ready to die. I *want* to die.' Possibly even, 'I deserve to die.' Brandon could still smell the evil and gunpowder in the air from that dark morning.

He looked down at the passage he'd found and read silently running a finger across the words:

*In the synagogue there was a man possessed by a demon, an impure spirit. He cried out at the top of his voice, "Go away! What do you want with us, Jesus of Nazareth? Have you come to destroy us? I know who you are—the Holy One of God!"*

*"Be quiet!" Jesus said sternly. "Come out of him!" Then the demon
throw the man down before them all and came out without injuring
him.*

Brandon looked up 'Mary Magdalene,' who his dad had said had
more than one demon. He found the text in Luke eight and read it:

*After this, Jesus traveled about from one town and village to another,
proclaiming the good news of the kingdom of God. The Twelve were
with him, and also some women who had been cured of evil spirits and
diseases: Mary (called Magdalene) from whom seven demons had
come out . . .*

Brandon kept reading and came to a scene where Jesus met a
demon-possessed man who lived among some tombs. When Jesus
asked the man's name, he replied, "Legion," because he was filled
with many demons.

A footnote in Brandon's Bible stated that Satan, the devil, is a
thief who comes to steal, kill, and destroy.

Brandon whispered "steal, kill, destroy" as he went to the
kitchen, grabbed a package of Oreos, and went back to the couch.

Inhaling cookie after cookie, he was led from one footnote and
passage to the next, reading about how Satan "entered" Judas
Iscariot just before he betrayed Jesus, and how Cain—"who was of
the evil one"—murdered his brother, Abel.

"Dang," Brandon whispered. "If this is true then demons really
do enter into certain people."

*Why?*

"To steal, kill, and destroy—not only the people they enter, but
those around them. Just like Gregory Newman. He killed those
people—and destroyed his marriage and family."

*Wait a second . . .*

He remembered his dad mentioned a scripture in the book of
Ephesians, about protecting yourself from demons. He tossed aside
the package of Oreo's and sat up on the edge of the couch. After
several minutes he finally found 'armor of God' and went to the
text in Ephesians six:

*Finally, be strong in the Lord and in his mighty power. Put on the full armor of God, so that you can take your stand against the devil's schemes. For our struggle is not against flesh and blood, but against the rulers, against the authorities, against the powers of this dark world and against the spiritual forces of evil in the heavenly realms.*

He read it a second time, slower, then slumped back on the couch with the Bible against his chest.

"So . . . we're not fighting people. We're fighting demons and evil spirits," Brandon whispered.

*Dang.*

It sounded like there was a whole host of evil beings and powers frolicking about, causing havoc in some unseen realm. And they wanted to *ruin* people. Brandon picked up reading where he'd left off:

*Therefore put on the full armor of God, so that when the day of evil comes, you may be able to stand your ground, and after you have done everything, to stand. Stand firm then, with the belt of truth buckled around your waist, with the breastplate of righteousness in place, and with your feet fitted with the readiness that comes from the gospel of peace. In addition to all this, take up the shield of faith, with which you can extinguish all the flaming arrows of the evil one."*

Brandon leaned back and closed his eyes. He wanted faith. He *needed* God in his life to do this job, to stand firm. "Help me, God. Help me have this armor and this shield. Give me the desire to find a church . . . to be closer to you."

He was finally tired.

He closed the Bible, grabbed the Oreos, and took them back to the kitchen, brushing the crumbs from the front of his hoodie. This time he took a big slug of milk from his half-gallon jug, then burped. All the thoughts about demons reminded him of the note Greg Newman left behind for his wife.

He quietly returned to his room, unplugged his phone, sat on the end of the bed, and found the glowing picture of the letter Greg had left for Jessica:

*Dear Jessica,*

*Ever since the day we met, you have been my world and the reason for my existence. I thought we were so happy.*

*As you know, I could not recover from the affair. I'm sorry, I tried. But the trust was gone. It was never coming back.*

*There is evil in this world, Jess. It came for you and now it's come for me. I think it comes for all people. I'm sorry it got the best of me. I'm sorry for the events of today.*

*I hope you will find someone who can help you rise above the evil and teach our children to do the same.*

*Please forget me now.*
*Gregory*

Brandon plugged the phone back in, stepped out of the flip-flops, threw the hoodie over a chair, and climbed into bed.

He stared up at the ceiling.

In several seconds, the light from the phone turned off and the room was black and silent.

Evil had come for Jessica—in the form of the affair.

And evil had come for Gregory—he'd killed two people, wounded three, and was gunned down himself.

And who was left?

Was it over?

Brandon's eyes closed and he began to drift off.

*Why had Christopher Dowdy cared so much in those first hours who the shooter had been?*

*Why had Dowdy said of Greg Newman, "I should have killed the twerp when I had the chance?"*

*Why had this whole sleepless night happened in the first place?*

*Maybe so you can stand firm . . . So you can extinguish the flaming arrows of the evil one.*

**19**

Deetz called Brandon from his car on the way into Police Bureau headquarters the following morning before 7 a.m. It was fifty degrees and steady rain.

"Hey, something's come up," Deetz said as he flipped his wipers to a higher speed. "Virgil got a call from Jackie Brooks, the woman who was shot on the plaza. She wants to talk to the investigators handling the Jumpy Jim's shooting. That's us."

"Did she say why?" Brandon said from his car.

"No, but Virgil said she called him early this morning and sounded really uptight. She said she's been wrestling with something ever since the shooting. She's already on her way in. She may be there when we get there."


Deetz arrived at headquarters before Brandon, and Virgil said he had Jackie Brooks set up in interrogation room B. He said she did not look well. Deetz hung up his wet coat, grabbed his pad and pen and thermal mug of 'Joanie' coffee, and ducked his head into the conference room.

At quick glance, the woman sitting opposite the metal table had a thin, ashen face with plumb-colored rings beneath her shifty eyes. Her shoulder-length dark blond hair had not been combed. She wore a wet purple raincoat and her arms were crossed tightly.

"Good morning." Deetz introduced himself and said he would be right back with his partner. But just then, he felt a tap on the shoulder from behind. It was Brandon, out of breath, taking his coat off.

Deetz whispered for Brandon to get a pad and pen, and coffee if he wanted. While he was gone, Deetz slipped into the interrogation room and took a seat across from Jackie Brooks, who asked if Deetz was related to J.P., with whom she worked at Jumpy Jim's. Deetz got it all out in the open right away that he was the father of both J.P. and Brandon.

Once they were all seated and introductions had been made, Deetz started the recorder on the table and stated the date, time, and who was in the interview.

"First of all, Mrs. Brooks, how are you doing, physically, since the shooting?" Deetz said. "It must've been horrific."

"Call me Jackie. Brooks is my married name." She shivered as she spoke. "I'm still in the process of getting it switched back to my maiden name. I'm divorced."

Deetz and Brandon nodded and waited.

"So, yeah . . . I'm fine. It went right through me, up here." With a trembling hand she touched her left shoulder. "The surgeon said it was a good thing I'm so skinny. The shot itself wasn't so bad, it's everything else." She huffed and her eyes shifted to the wall, then the ceiling, as if she was holding back tears.

"It's good you're okay," Deetz said. "We were going to speak with you, eventually, but thank you for coming in. Let's first get to what you wanted to talk to us about."

Jackie rocked back and forth briefly, blew out audibly through the corner of her mouth, and wrapped a handful of tangled hair behind her right ear. "The night before the shooting, Sunday night, I got a text message—from Alexander Dowdy." As Dowdy's name left her mouth, Jackie's face contorted and she cried. But she kept going. "He wanted me to come in early. Seven a.m. I usually come in at eight or eight-thirty." She stopped suddenly and pressed trembling fingers to her lips.

To lighten things up, Deetz said, "What is your job at Jumpy Jim's, Jackie?"

"Techie. I'm a techie. I help with online ads, marketing, search optimization. That's how I know J.P. He's over that."

"What was Dowdy's reason for wanting you in early, do you know?" Brandon said.

Jackie shook her head several times. "He never said. I just said yes, because, well, he's at the top of the food chain. When he or his son calls a meeting, you're there."

"Okay, that is definitely good to know," Deetz said. "What else did you want to tell us—before we walk through what happened that morning?"

Jackie cursed under her breath and dropped her head, a small hand cupping her forehead as if she had a migraine.

"It's okay, Jackie, take your time." Deetz glanced at Brandon, who was on the edge of his chair as if he was watching a thriller movie.

Suddenly, Jackie's metal chair shoved backward, making an awful screeching noise, and she was on her feet with her arms crossed so tightly it looked like she was in a straight-jacket. She was wire thin.

She paced. When she wasn't looking at them, Deetz nodded at Brandon with a hand up, signaling to be patient, to wait for her to speak.

Jackie stopped in the corner of the small room, put her hand on her waist, and began speaking without looking at the officers. "Christopher Dowdy drugged me. And I believe he may have raped me. I didn't report it because, when I confronted him about it the following week, he denied it ever happened and said I would be terminated if 'rumors of that sort' were even mentioned."

Deetz and Brandon absorbed the shock in silence.

Deetz's mind spun. They had to take this one step at a time.

"When and where did the incident happen?"

She tapped her foot on the floor repeatedly, arms still crossed. "Two months ago. He knew I'd been recently divorced and asked if I wanted to meet up one night. I knew he was married, but . . . I don't know what got into me." She closed her eyes and continued. "We had drinks and appetizers at Sergio's. I had too much to drink."

Jackie retrieved a tissue from her bag, excused herself, blew her nose, and sat back down at the table across from Deetz and Brandon.

"I woke up in the middle of the night in my bed. My head was spinning, I mean *spinning*. I was weak. Totally confused. My vision was blurred. And it was not from the alcohol. I've been drunk before. This was *drugs*. I've done my research. I think it was Rohypnol or possibly Ketamine."

Deetz knew those to be 'date rape' drugs.

Brandon scribbled furiously.

Deetz jotted down questions that he didn't want to forget to ask.

"Did Dowdy have a key to your place?" Brandon said.

"No, but of course I had it with me. I figure he brought us back to my place and got us in with my key. I don't remember any of it."

"Then what?" Deetz said.

Jackie's jaw clenched.

"I woke up at three-thirty in the morning. I got sick. I was wearing the outfit I had on that night, but I could tell he'd removed my clothes and put them back on. A strap on my bra was twisted and my shirt was buttoned unevenly. I was so sick I had to call in and take off work that day. My mind was a complete fog for at least twenty-four hours."

"You didn't report this to the police?" Brandon said.

She shook her head. "I was scared. I can't lose this job." She began to cry.

"You said earlier you think he *may have* raped you . . ." Deetz said.

She took in a deep breath, her face tinged with embarrassment. She sighed. "I was . . . there was some sign of that, I think. And I may've been sore . . . But I'm just not sure anymore. But I couldn't go on without saying anything because I'm about to go insane." Her shoulders shook and her head dropped as she sobbed as quietly as she could.

"Mrs. Brooks, er, Jackie, you really should have called the police. We would have had you tested," Deetz said. "He would have been charged."

She shot to her feet again. "I know, I know. I'm sorry." She crossed to the corner of the small room, pounded the wall, and ran both hands through her hair. "I'm such a coward. I just didn't. I don't know why. I didn't do the right thing. I regret it."

"Tell us what happened when you confronted him," Deetz said.

"Ha. When I went to his office he smiled and welcomed me in as if nothing had ever happened. He even brought it up first, laughing about how much I'd had to drink. He said he'd taken me home, put me in my bed, and left. When I told him I was dizzy and sick, that I thought I'd been drugged and my clothes had been changed—oh my gosh, he got *livid*. He raced over, slammed his office door, and berated me. He was within inches of my face. Threatened to fire me if I spread such rumors. I still can't believe it. It doesn't seem real."

Her hands trembled in the prayer position against her mouth as she seemed to be reliving the whole thing in her mind.

"Jackie," Deetz snapped her out of it. "Was anything else said about it between the two of you?"

She shook her head quickly. 'No. No way. I've even questioned myself, thinking maybe I was just drunk and what he said was true. I've not been in a good place . . . since the divorce. And now this shooting. My life's never going to be the same."

"Did you ever find out what the meeting was supposed to be about—that Alexander Dowdy called you in early for? I mean, did he ever tell you?" Brandon said.

"We haven't been back," Jackie said. "Will Tomason, one of the owners, announced right after it happened that we were closing Monday and Tuesday. And Wednesday through Friday would be optional. I'm not going back until Monday."

"Are you okay walking us through what happened when you got to work Monday morning?" Deetz said.

Jackie cleared her throat and set her shoulders back. "I parked where I always do, in the employee lot to the west of the complex. I walked over like I always do, across the plaza. The first thing I saw from a distance was a police car and then beyond that was Greg's car, and I immediately thought, 'Wait a minute, what's his car doing out there?' You don't park there."

She paused and sniffed and wiped her nose with a fresh tissue.

"As I got closer, I saw the officer was talking to Greg. I slowed down. I wasn't sure what was going on, but it didn't look dangerous. I mean, you know, this was a co-worker, conversing with a cop."

She rolled her eyes and dropped back in the chair. "Before I know it, Greg's got a gun. The cop draws his gun. Greg is yelling for the cop to leave. I was in shock. I froze. Right then, the cop turned and yelled at me to run and Greg just shot him, just like that, with no warning." She cried. "Oh my gosh, he was bleeding so badly. I ran. Greg called my name and came running after me. He was so fast! I heard him say he was sorry—then I got shot. It felt like someone shoved me really hard."

"Did Greg say any more to you? Or do you remember exactly what he said?" Deetz said.

"He called my name several times. He said he was sorry. Oh my gosh, his voice was just . . . I don't know, anguished. That's all I can remember. And, no, once I got shot, he was gone. I heard other shots, glass shattering, I guess from when he entered the building. Another officer showed up soon, and the medics."

"You've been through a lot," Deetz said. "We're almost finished."

Jackie's head dropped and she nodded.

"Did you see any indicators at work, any warning signs, anything out of the ordinary with Greg Newman?"

"I knew there was tension between Greg and Christopher Dowdy, but there was tension anyway throughout, ever since Dowdy came in to run the company."

"How did you know there was tension between Greg and Dowdy?" Deetz said.

"They would get into it. Little arguments here and there. It was obvious they didn't like each other. But Dowdy is like sandpaper. That's just his personality. The whole company culture has changed since he's been there. It used to be more like a family. Now it's . . . well, who knows now?"

"You didn't know Greg had guns?" Deetz said. "You never heard threats that would have indicated this was coming?"

"Not at all. Greg is one of the last people I would have expected to do something like this."

"Jackie," Brandon said, "we believe Greg was looking for Dowdy during the rampage. Do you have any idea, even a guess, as to why Greg would want to kill Christopher Dowdy?"

## 20

Deetz knew Brandon didn't like Christopher Dowdy from the start, so his question to Jackie Brooks toward the end of the interview didn't surprise him. In fact, Deetz was glad he'd asked it. It couldn't hurt.

Jackie's delay in answering was curious. She sat there for the longest time, looking down at the tissue she was fidgeting with in her hands on the table between her and the officers.

Her eyes flicked up to Deetz, then to Brandon.

"Dowdy had an affair with Greg's wife, Jessica," she said.

Deetz nodded. "We are aware of that."

The room was silent.

Jackie looked at the window in the door, then back at the officers.

"Carrie Sandowski, the woman who was killed in our office . . ." Jackie stopped talking, leaned onto the table, and rocked back and forth as if she was a patient in a nursing home. "If I say something that gets Dowdy in trouble, will I have to appear in court, like testify, publicly?"

Deetz and Brandon glanced at each other.

"It depends what it is," Deetz said. "The bottom line, Jackie, is that we need you to tell us everything you know—and to tell the truth. If Christopher Dowdy broke the law or somehow brought on what happened Monday, he needs to be held accountable."

"Carrie and I were friends," Jackie blurted. "We worked together a lot on our website and the online store, so we got close. Anyway, I told her about what I told you, about that night with Dowdy. Then she told me something."

Jackie took in a deep breath and blew out through the corner of her mouth again. "She said Dowdy threatened her, tried to coerce into having sex."

As Jackie searched for another tissue in her bag, Deetz seethed. And he could tell by the look on Brandon's face that he was feeling the same angst toward Dowdy once again.

"He called her into his office late one afternoon, shut the door, sat at his desk, and asked her to go to some happy hour with him," Jackie said. "She told him she was engaged and he said he knew that. And he just sat there, smirking, waiting for an answer. She said it was *so* awkward and just so unbelievable, she didn't know what to do. It was pure harassment. Finally, she said she was sorry, but it wouldn't be right for her to go, and she turned to leave. But he ran over to the door and stopped her, actually physically got in her way."

Deetz glanced over and Brandon's face was on fire. The justice-lover in him was about to explode.

"Carrie actually told me she feared for her safety right at that moment," Jackie said. "So at the door he looks at her and says, 'If you want to keep your job, you'll change your mind. I'll give you a week.' Then he threw the door open and said, 'Close the door behind you.'"

"And what happened in a week?" Brandon said.

Jackie looked at them both and shook her head. "This Thursday would be one week."

Deetz and Brandon looked at each other.

"That's pretty much it." Jackie wiped her nose again.

"Well we can't thank you enough for—"

"Oh, one more thing," she held up an index finger in the hand that clutched the tissue. "Carrie got the same text I did Sunday night from Alexander Dowdy, to be in at seven."

. . .

WHEN DEETZ and Brandon finished the meeting with Jackie Brooks, they were called into Sergeant Dolby Tidwell's office, where they were invited to sit with Tidwell, Virgil, and Assistant Head of Homicide Sid Sikorski.

Deetz and Brandon spent the next ten minutes updating their colleagues on everything they'd found out thus far in the investigation.

"I'm going to postpone the meeting with Dowdy that was set for later this morning," Deetz said. "Number one, it's pouring and he wanted to meet outside, Eastbank Esplanade. Number two, we're not ready for him. I've got to spend more time on questions. Especially after all we just learned from Jackie Brooks."

"Okay, good," Tidwell said. "We've got some new intel for you as well. Sid?"

"Yeah guys, you won't believe this. We got a call a little while ago from a guy from Beaverton by the name of Sam Friend." Sid cleared his throat, swiveled in his chair, and tapped repeatedly at the screen of his iPad. "Sam Friend recognized Greg Newman from the shooting, from the news, and said he had something to show us."

Sid shoved his chair back, got up, and waved the iPad as he spoke. "Believe it or not, what you're about to see happened at Eastbank Esplanade. So, if Christopher Dowdy wanted to meet you there today, it must be one of his favorite spots. Anyway, last week Sam Friend was at Eastbank eating his lunch at a picnic table when he saw an argument break out and, like any good citizen, he videotaped it on his phone."

Sid leaned over onto the table between Deetz and Brandon so they could both see his screen.

Tidwell's phone vibrated. He glanced at it and stood. "I've got to handle something. Virgil, I think I'm gonna need you. We've seen that already," Tidwell said, pointing at the iPad. "Looks like there may be more to the shooting than meets the eye. Dig into it, guys. Let me know if you need anything."

Tidwell and Virgil left the room, then Virgil ducked his head back in. "I forgot to tell you guys, the service for Danny is Friday morning at Peace Gardens. Processional will start here at nine o'clock sharp," Virgil said. "Spread the word. We want a good turnout for the family. We'll have mourning bands for everyone to wear. There's also a GoFundMe page, just search his name."

Deetz jotted a note to himself and Virgil took off.

"Okay, here we go," Sid said. "Listen closely. It's windy, but you can pick up some of the audio."

Sid punched 'play' and Deetz and Brandon leaned closer to the iPad.

The screen showed two men face-to-face on the lawn of the park yelling at each other, the Willamette River in the background. One of the men, the shorter of the two, was clearly Gregory Newman, wearing khaki pants and a navy windbreaker. The video was slightly grainy and appeared to have been shot from about fifty feet away, and the audio picked up the humming sound of a constant breeze.

"That's Christopher Dowdy!" Brandon said, pointing at the other man, the taller of the two, wearing black workout shorts, a white Nike jacket, white sunglasses and, of course, his signature Bluetooth earpiece.

"And Greg Newman," Sid said. "Keep watching. Listen."

Deetz was rigid. He could only swallow and watch breathlessly.

Sid said quietly, "Sam Friend told us he started recording this after Greg Newman had already taken a swing at Dowdy."

In the video, Dowdy spoke forcefully to Greg Newman, punching an index finger in his chest repeatedly. Then Greg exploded in a rage and shoved Dowdy, yelling at him like a mad man, his head wagging. But Dowdy was a much larger man, heavier, and barely budged. He put both hands up, nodded and spoke, as if to calm Greg. But then, out of nowhere, Dowdy threw a sweeping backhand slap to Greg's face, which snapped his head back and sent his glasses flying.

"Unbelievable," Brandon whispered.

Greg immediately bent over in search of his glasses with his back to Dowdy. He was crouching so low it appeared he was virtually blind without them. Deetz had a sick hunch what was coming next and, sure enough, Dowdy lifted a knee high and booted Greg in the rear as hard as he could, sending him face first into the wet grass, his arms outstretched as if he was diving into a pool.

The video footage jiggled as Sam Friend adjusted the camera, temporarily showing a concrete picnic table, half-eaten pita sandwich and pickle. When the viewfinder found the two men again it was from a bit closer distance. Greg Newman was crawling in the thick grass, patting around frantically for his glasses as Dowdy walked step-by-step behind him, yelling the whole time.

"Now listen," Sid said.

The audio was still mostly the constant breeze, but several words of Dowdy's rant could be understood in between wind gusts: "You're weak . . . never be . . . lowlife accountant . . . laughingstock . . ."

Dowdy's rulership over Greg infuriated Deetz.

Greg finally found his black glasses and, leaning on his elbows in the grass, put them back on his face with trembling hands.

Deetz felt an aching pity for Greg Newman and a growing hatred toward Dowdy.

Greg put a hand on the ground and one knee up to begin standing and, without a word, Dowdy kicked him in the gut with such force that Greg dropped flat to the ground on his face.

Sam Friend walked the camera seven or eight steps closer to the beating.

"I . . . your wife, Greg! You can't trust her . . . Women . . . office think you're a loser . . . Jackie Brooks, Carrie . . . laugh at you when they're with me . . . closed doors." Dowdy ranted in a jesting, demeaning tone.

Greg rolled over, sat on the ground rocking, trying to get air in his lungs. He looked as if he might lunge at Dowdy's legs.

". . . want to keep your . . . overpriced salary . . . exactly what I say . . . pay who I say . . ."

Greg replied something unintelligible.

Dowdy's head snapped back in surprise and he roared with laughter.

Then Greg ripped a gun from his coat pocket.

Dowdy's face sobered instantly and his hands shot up.

Sam Friend's camera slowly backed away, but he kept videotaping.

Greg worked his way to his feet while pointing the gun at Dowdy's chest and talking as he did so. Dowdy tried to say something, but Greg yelled spastically for him to shut up, raised the gun higher, and stepped closer to Dowdy. As Greg spoke more he nodded and smiled, but only a few sporadic words could be deciphered. ". . . recording this . . . all your threats . . ."

Sam Friend walked the camera closer to the two men, perhaps so he could more clearly capture what was being said.

That's when Greg Newman noticed the videographer's movement out the corner of his eye—and turned to look at him.

In a flash, Christopher Dowdy snatched the gun from Greg's hand, shoved it into his throat, grabbed the neck of Greg's jacket in a fist and brought the smaller man close to him. Dowdy glanced at the cameraman—who retreated several steps—but returned his focus to Greg, speaking harshly through clenched teeth, his words inaudible.

Greg shook his head and held up both hands innocently, but Dowdy wasn't buying it. He spun Greg around and forced him to his knees. With the gun pressed to the back of Greg's neck, Dowdy patted the man down with his free hand. Within seconds he pulled a cell phone from the breast pocket of Greg's jacket and examined it.

Dowdy slowly looked from the cell phone screen down at Greg, then raised the phone in the air and cracked it over the kneeling man's skull.

"Get out of here," Brandon whispered. "This guy's a maniac."

"Shhh," Deetz said.

Greg Newman wilted to the ground.

Dowdy said something to him, then trotted toward the water and hurled the phone like a shot putter into the Willamette River.

As he stomped back toward Greg, Dowdy pointed the gun at the videographer, Sam Friend, and spit out an unintelligible tirade.

That's when the footage went black as Sam Friend jammed the phone in his pocket and ran for his life.

## 21

BRANDON'S BLOOD boiled as he sat there with Deetz and Sid at the table in Sergeant Tidwell's office. Yes, Greg Newman had gone off the handle and killed innocent people in J.P.'s office complex—it was horrific, cowardly, and unthinkable. But, from all they'd learned, Christopher Dowdy seemed equally as sinister.

"You okay?" Deetz whispered.

Brandon nodded sharply and scribbled on his pad.

"Cool down," Deetz said. "We'll get to the bottom of it."

Brandon nodded and asked Sid when the video of Greg Newman and Christopher Dowdy had been shot.

"Last Wednesday. So, two days before Greg Newman was fired." Sid stood and gathered his things. "Also, the lab says Newman did a military grade erase of the hard drive on his laptop, so that's a blank. We're still working on his desktop computer from work. When we learn any more, you boys will be the first to know." They thanked him and he left the office.

Deetz looked at Brandon. "I can tell you're frustrated."

"I just can't believe how some people treat other human beings." Brandon glanced at his dad and down at the table. "It's despicable." Brandon couldn't get the images of Dowdy bullying Newman out of his mind.

"Yeah." Deetz sighed. "After a while you get numb to it. I don't know if that's good or bad."

"I couldn't sleep last night," Brandon said softly. "I read about demons."

"Yeah?"

"It said we don't fight against flesh and blood. It's almost like it's saying, 'Hey, you guys, remember your enemy isn't Greg Newman or Christopher Dowdy or whoever—it's Satan who's driving them. It's like some whole unseen war going on."

Deetz touched Brandon's wrist and their eyes locked. With emotion swelling up in his eyes, Deetz said, "That's right, son. And the thing we need to cling to is . . . there's a verse I learned a long time ago. 'The fear of man brings a snare, but the one who trusts in the Lord will be protected.' That word 'protected' also means safe, secure, set on high."

Brandon's lips pursed and he felt tears well up in his eyes. The whole thing was infuriating and confusing and depressing. He didn't want his dad to see his emotions and he turned away.

"God has us, Brandon," Deetz whispered. "He knows our job. He knows we're trying to do good. He's fighting with us—against the evil. I believe that."

"But why does he allow it in the first place?" Brandon snapped and turned back to Deetz. "Good cops like us die, dad. Danny Rodriguez is dead and his kids don't have a father. I just don't get it. Christopher Dowdy is ruining peoples' lives and he's out there walking around free. Why is God okay with that?"

"God is not okay with that and we can do something about it, son. We can interrogate Dowdy and get the district attorney involved—"

"And what's he going to get, three years? Two?"

Deetz dropped his head, probably because he knew it may be true.

Brandon couldn't recall a time he'd ever felt so much disgust toward another human being as he did Christopher Dowdy.

Deetz slowly looked up at Brandon. "We have to remember what you just said. Our fight isn't against Dowdy. It's against the powers that rule him."

Brandon shook his head and looked down. "If God is love and God is powerful, then why? I can't think of one good reason he would allow Dowdy to have an affair with Newman's wife, or allow

Dowdy to drug-rape Jackie Brooks, or sexually-harass Carrie Sandowski. It's complete carnage. Their lives are all ruined, or over."

"Look, I don't claim to have an answer, son. I *don't* have one. The Bible says down here on earth we see in a mirror dimly and we know only in part, but one day we'll see clearly, we'll know fully. I guess that's why they call it 'faith.' Sometimes we don't understand and we just have to trust that God knows best."

Deep down, Brandon believed that, but it was very deep down.

Once again, he silently marveled, not only at his dad's knowledge of the scriptures, but at his unblinking confidence in an unseen God.

Compared to his dad, Brandon's walk with God was barren.

He wanted that to change. He *needed* it to change if he was going to keep his sanity working for the Portland Police.

Deetz turned a page on his pad and pushed up his sleeves. "Let's go over where we are and what we need to do next, okay?"

"Get Dowdy in here for questioning," Brandon blurted.

"Right, for sure. And we need to be super-prepared for that. The thing is, I'd like to have more evidence. Carrie Sandowski is dead so the story Jackie told about her sexual harassment is just that, a story. Jackie's account of her drug-rape, well, that's a story too at this point. There's no evidence."

"Dad, come on, this guy's a maniac. The longer he's—"

"That's why I think we need to talk to a couple other people first, to get what we need to really put the clamps to him."

"Who?"

"His wife and his dad."

## 22

Deetz heard a commotion in the hallway outside the interrogation room, saw several officers run past, and suddenly the door burst open. Detective Angie Cook stuck her ashen face in with her brown eyes the size of quarters. "All hands on deck out front," Angie said. "Patriots are having a rally, a protest, whatever you want to call it. Trouble's brewing. Sarge wants everyone out there."

She was gone.

Deetz and Brandon left their things, grabbed their coats, and dashed up the steps to the front entrance of Portland Police Bureau headquarters. Deetz led the way outside where they were hit by a cold drizzle beneath dark gray skies.

"People are afraid to come to Portland," came a blaring, amplified male voice. "They're afraid to stay in our hotels, eat in our restaurants, visit our museums, go to our churches, and walk in our parks! Who can blame them?"

The man yelling through a white and red megaphone was Woody Galt, one of the organizers of the Patriots. He was rough-looking, about forty, with a brown beard and a boxer's smashed nose.

Deetz nodded for Brandon to follow him, and they joined a growing number of officers at the bottom of the steps who were forming a human barricade.

Dozens of passersby had stopped to listen.

"This city has become unsafe—*dangerous*—as a direct result of the actions of Mayor Barbara Meeks and City Council." The megaphone turned Galt's voice into a mechanical echo that pierced the damp, dark morning air. "Let's just come out and say it! This wasn't happening before they took office!"

Galt was surrounded by a motley crowd of some seventy to ninety bulked up Patriots, many with tattoos, wearing goggles and flak jackets, and waving American and confederate flags. One held a sign that showed a picture of an AK-47 rifle with the words, 'Come and Take It.' Other signs and flags read: 'God Bless America,' 'Enough Is Enough,' 'If You Are Here Illegally, Go Home,' and 'Don't Tread On Me.'

"Stay here," Deetz said to Brandon. "We need helmets and shields. I'll be right back."

Taking two steps at a time, Deetz rushed back inside and searched for any officer in command. He found Ben Briggs in the midst of a tense radio conversation.

"We need riot gear out there," Deetz interrupted.

"It's coming," Ben said. "SERT should be here."

"We didn't know about this?"

Ben shook his head and covered the radio. "Negative. It was on nobody's radar. And they didn't tell us."

"I don't have a good feeling." Deetz hurried back out and saw that a black SERT truck had arrived and officers in riot gear were filing out the back doors. Several SERT team members passed helmets and shields down the line of officers forming the barricade.

The Portland Patriots were a group of outspoken locals who'd formed after becoming fed up with Portland's liberal government and media, and the violent protests of left-wing liberals. They were flag-toting, gun-loving, freedom-embracing citizens of all ages and races who believed in limited government and sided with local law enforcement. Brandon had once considered joining their efforts, but Deetz had talked him down. *Thank God.*

Two news trucks from different stations arrived at the same time from different directions.

Tension mounted by the second and Deetz was thinking they needed as many bodies as they could get down front.

"We are seeing the fruits of the mayor's massive police budget cuts and City Council's mandate ordering police to stand down in the face of criminal behavior—and people, it ain't good fruit," Galt yelled. "We want all Portlanders to know what's really happening. People, do you know our police are no longer allowed to pull over suspicious vehicles? It's true. And did you know our police are not allowed to share videos to the American people of the riots happening in our streets and neighborhoods?"

Many of the Patriots yelled and screamed and waved in agreement.

The dozens of bystanders had quickly turned into hundreds, many of whom were yelling back at the Patriots in anger.

Deetz spotted a large mob three blocks away, descending on police headquarters like a cloud of locusts. He got Brandon's attention and nodded toward them, and whispered, "Buckle up." Brandon mumbled something and tightened the chin strap on his helmet.

"This is ludicrous!" Galt continued. "Our community is sick and tired of the mobs, riots, violence, and criminal destruction. We want our city back! And we want our police back! They need to have the power, authority, and *budget* to restore order and protect the citizens of this city."

That brought boos from many of the onlookers, who were bumping right up along the line of officers.

As the mob drew closer Deetz could see that many of their faces were covered with sunglasses, ski masks, helmets, hoods, scarves, and bandanas. Most wore black from head to booted feet, and carried baseball bats, chains, black and red flags, and signs that read, 'White Supremacy is Terrorism,' 'Feds Go Home,' 'White Silence Kills,' 'End Police Brutality,' and 'Trans Lives Matter.'

All Deetz could think about was how much Brandon had already endured as a rookie officer this week—and now he had to deal with this drama.

"You've all seen this is a peaceful gathering," Galt called as the mob of Patriot opponents made their way through the crowd right up to the line of officers at the human barricade. "But watch what happens. We're about to see what they've become known for— wanton anarchy! Is that what you want, Portland? Is that what you want, America? *Wake up!* It's time to take our country back!"

Deetz yelled to Brandon as they stood side-by-side with their comrades, "Watch the people in the back. They'll be the ones throwing things."

A woman in all black with a rainbow armband and the body of a construction worker got right in Brandon's face. She wore a black scarf, hood, and sunglasses. Her sign read, 'Anti-Fascist Zone.' Every other word out of her yelling, spitting mouth was the F-bomb.

Deetz noted that Brandon's legs and body were locked and loaded. He wasn't about to be moved. As the woman screamed in his face and wagged her head, the expression on his face was one of both distress and wrath.

Deetz was relieved to see another SERT truck inching its way through the growing crowd to the east, and, within seconds, re-enforcements were jumping out the back like a domino of paratroopers.

*Good.*

Deetz saw a small rock fly past, then a brick which smashed the concrete steps behind them. A cloud of orange tear gas or pepper spray arose and floated in the misty air some fifteen rows back. Fireworks exploded around them and people screamed.

"Keep it safe," Deetz yelled to Brandon. "Just deescalate. Don't let them get to you."

"Yeah, don't let us get to you—you filthy *pig!*" the woman screamed in Brandon's face.

He clenched his teeth and his cheeks darkened, then he shoved his shield toward her and yelled, "Stay back!"

*Help him keep his cool . . . protect us.*

That incited the woman and she pounded on Brandon's shield repeatedly and screamed obscenities as if she'd lost her sanity. Other protesters began to do the same down the line, including a smaller woman near them who wore all black, including a motorcycle helmet, leather gloves, and steel-toed Doc Martins.

"Ma'am, stay back!" Deetz yelled at the woman who was taunting Brandon. "There's no need to hit. Keep it peaceful. *Stop!*"

Just then, Deetz's shield was bashed by a heavy flying object.

It jolted him and hurt his wrist, but he managed to hold onto the shield.

He was confused and didn't know what had hit him.

He looked down at the pavement.

A plastic bag had hit the shield and dropped to the ground.

The bag had split open upon impact.

His shield was covered in liquid, which was dripping to the ground.

He couldn't figure out what it was.

Then he smelled it.

*Urine.*

He felt his face contort in disgust.

His first reaction was to look at Brandon, hoping he hadn't seen.

But he had seen.

Brandon was staring straight at Deetz with his mouth open. Then, slowly, his face morphed into a grotesque mask of fury.

Brandon blurted an expletive and asked if his dad was okay.

"I'm fine. Forget it," Deetz called. "Just protect yourself. Stay cool."

But as Brandon turned back visibly seething at the raucous mob, his dark eyes darting about the crowd for the culprit, Deetz wondered for the first time whether his son had the temperament for the job—especially amidst Portland's rampant cancel culture.

**23**
___________

"Tell me more about why you wanted to meet, Brandon? I know you've had a heck of a week. Talk to me a little bit." Dr. Terri Wallender sat across from Brandon in her plush, lamp-lit downtown office late in the afternoon the same day of the morning riot. Brandon was still in uniform on his way home. His stomach growled.

"I'm just . . . I'm *mad*," he said. "How dare they throw urine at us. *Sick*. And it hit my dad! He's sixty years old. He doesn't deserve that. I'm just frustrated. If this is what this job is going to be about, I'm having second thoughts."

Dr. Wallender jotted something down on the small pad in her lap. Her brown hair was cut short. She wore brown slacks and a matching jacket, with a crisp white button-down shirt. Pearl necklace and earrings. Thick black belt and black heels.

"You said the last time we met that you were somewhat worried about your dad being back in uniform."

"Well, today, yeah. I felt sorry for him. I just . . . when he got hit, I could've killed someone, I was so angry. I mean, seriously, I wasn't positive I was going to be able to control myself. That's why I'm here. I'm not supposed to take sides. Our job in that situation is to keep people safe while we try to let them express themselves."

"Was it difficult for you not to take sides?"

"Oh my gosh, heck yeah. If we're being honest right now, by all

116

means, I would take the side of the Patriots. They back the Blue. They believe in law and order. You should have seen the other side. They hate our guts! Why? What have we ever done to them except keep them safe?"

"Well, just to talk through that point, many of them, I believe, are protesting because of the George Floyd murder, and many other racially-motivated atrocities like it through the centuries. You know that."

"But they're stereotyping *me*. That woman who was pounding on my shield and spitting at us, she doesn't know me! She could care less about my feelings. The hatred was just palpable."

"Uh huh. But you understand, the other side is trying to say that racism is ingrained in our culture, that we are taught it from a young age. They want change."

"What is this? You agree with them?"

"This is not about me, Brandon. I'm trying to help you understand their side so you can—"

"I understand their side. You know what one of the signs said today? 'Another World Is Possible.' It's not just about race, it's about gender, it's about sexual preference. Race is only part of it. They want to shove their beliefs down our throats. You want another world? Move to another country!"

Her head tilted, her dark eyebrows lifted, and she waited.

That's what shrinks did, they waited. Their job was to get you to spill your guts. Brandon wanted to, and he had been assured this was a safe place to do so.

"You want to know what I think?" he continued.

"By all means, that's what I'm here for," she said in a tone that sounded slightly condescending.

"No, really, I've thought about this a lot. I think a lot of these protestors are embarrassed or ashamed of their own lifestyles. They silently hate themselves for the way they live, or the choices they've made, and because of their guilt, they're trying to force their beliefs on the rest of society, thinking that's going to make it acceptable. But it's not. It never will. That kind of hatred is never going to win anyone over."

"Hmm." Dr. Wallender's mouth sealed. She blinked slowly and nodded, then frowned. Her wheels were turning. "You obviously have some emotional opinions on all this. The bottom line is that you can't allow yourself to succumb to the hatred and the emotions flying at these protests—"

"They're more like riots."

"My point is, it's in your police laws and directives that officers remain neutral and unbiased. When you're on that line, you can't be thinking about what those people are saying. Your job is to constantly be looking ahead for criminal behavior, active threats, weapons, homemade weapons, explosives. You need to be focused on trying to anticipate if someone is planning any kind of violent behavior, like driving a vehicle into the crowd or something."

"I get all that. That's what I was trying to do."

"And it sounds like you did very well. Brandon, think about what you've faced this week. You witnessed a horrible, ghastly scene downtown on Monday, where you were forced to shoot a man who died. This was your job, and you did what you were supposed to do, by the book. And then today you were on the front lines of an extremely dangerous and venomous exchange, about which you obviously have some very strong personal feelings."

Brandon tented his hands in front of his face.

"And what makes all that even more traumatic and pressure-packed is the fact that your dad was with you, right by your side, in both instances."

Brandon nodded and fought back a surge of emotion. Partnering with his dad had definitely added to the stress factor.

"But you did tell me that you made it through the protest okay, that you did indeed, keep your cool—"

"I wouldn't say I kept my cool. I kept myself from physically hurting those idiots."

"And you know what, Brandon? Bravo for you." She leaned forward and spoke from the heart. "You did your job out there today and then you had the wherewithal to talk about it with your counselor. The Bureau needs more men and women like you. Remember, this is all new to you, brand new! Starting any new job is stressful, but especially this job, and especially this week."

Brandon inhaled deeply and sighed.

"It's going to take time, months, to get used to this job," she said. "Crowd control is one of the most complex situations you'll ever face. It's a shame you have to face it at all, but unfortunately it's become a big part of the job."

She didn't come out and say it, but Brandon knew Dr. Wallender was referring to the fact that every single member of the Bureau's Rapid Response Team had quit months ago during all of the political turmoil. They had extensive training and experience in crowd control, and now regular officers were doing their jobs.

"I guess one of the reasons I wanted to talk to you is because I'm bothered by all the anger in the world," Brandon said. "I don't remember it being this way when I was a kid. People would talk through things. Now it's pick a side—a far right or far left side— and go to war. Like today, both those groups were way right and way left. Is there no common-sense middle ground anymore?"

"That's a good point," she said softly. "The thing about being police, though, is that you're called to be neutral, to respect all people."

"This morning we watched a citizen's videotape that was shot from his phone." Brandon swallowed back his emotions. He couldn't believe he was telling her this, but he desperately wanted to get it off his chest. "It showed a man physically and mentally beating down another man, just demoralizing him."

She nodded and waited.

"It turned out the man being beaten was the shooter—from Monday. The one I killed."

"Oh, dear," she said. "Wow."

"Yeah."

"How did the video of that argument make you feel?"

Brandon's head dropped and he fought back tears. "I felt sorry for him. I could almost understand why he did what he did, but obviously that's not right. We can't think like that. It's just, it feels like everyone's temper is ramped up to the boiling point. Even mine. I'm part of the problem."

She gave a slight smile. "Believe me, working in law enforcement in today's culture is going to take a lot of getting used to," she said. "It's major stress. It's traumatic on the mind, soul, and spirit. It requires endless patience and discretion. I'm not telling you anything you haven't learned from your father and from the Academy."

Brandon nodded.

He liked Dr. Wallender.

It felt good to speak honestly with an anonymous third party.

He was comfortable in her office, she was a beautiful woman, and he wanted to stay longer.

Dr. Wallender tapped her pen to her pad. "You said last time you were looking for a church or some sort of small group. Have you found something?"

*Ugh.*

He'd put it off and put it off, and her words reminded him of his disappointment in himself. He was an adult now, and he'd failed to make his faith a priority.

"No. Unfortunately . . . no," he said, sheepishly. "I really want to, I just haven't had time. This was my senior year of college, plus I did Basic Academy, so it's been busy, to say the least."

"Well, I'm not prescribing faith or church or religion, but since you said that was important to you and to your family, I'm thinking it may be good for you—mentally and spiritually."

"You're right, for sure." He got the vibe she was bringing it to an end so he stood, rather abruptly. "Thanks a lot for your time. I hope I didn't get too heavy."

"Not at all." She stood, dropped her pad in the chair, and walked toward the door. "I'm glad you wanted to talk. This is a safe place for you, Brandon. You really have been through a lot for your first week. Don't hesitate to come in again whenever you need."

He nodded and stepped past her, through the door, smelling the mesmerizing scent of her perfume.

Dear goodness, she was beautiful.

Hesitantly, he stopped and turned to face her. "Thank you, again."

"You're welcome. You stay safe out there, okay?"

"You, too." He instantly realized his gaffe and his face ignited with embarrassment. She chuckled and he walked away feeling like a schoolboy with a crush on his teacher.

**24**

_______

Deetz was feeling surprisingly clear and sharp considering the hellacious day they'd had at the Patriot protest the day before. Brandon was eating a smelly Taco Bell breakfast burrito as he steered the Interceptor toward the downtown high-rise where Christopher and Darlene Dowdy lived.

After the nerve-racking day Deetz had put in, Joanie had insisted he have a good dinner and turn in early, so he'd logged almost nine hours of sleep. He'd gone for an early run in the neighborhood that morning and they'd enjoyed breakfast together.

"Your mom helped me come up with some of the questions for this interview," Deetz said as he clutched a mug of Joanie's coffee in his lap. "She thinks of things from a woman's perspective; she would have made a good investigator."

Brandon's phone vibrated. He glanced at it. "What? J.P.'s back at work. I knew he couldn't wait."

"Already?" Deetz said. "I thought he was taking the week off."

"Apparently not." Brandon swung the police SUV into a parking deck off Simonton Ave. He grabbed a ticket at the gate and began to drive up and around to find a place to park.

"J.P. said Dowdy's at work now, so I guess that's good," Brandon said.

"Yeah, we'll have his wife alone. Eleventh floor."

"Right."

They found a spot and parked, grabbed their stuff, and Deetz led them toward the elevators and a set of double doors, texting Darlene Dowdy as they walked.

"This should be interesting," Brandon said, tossing his burrito wrapper in a trash can outside the glass doors.

"Can you do me a favor and record it on your phone?" Deetz said.

"Yeah, is yours not working?"

"It is. I just want to be able to focus on the questions. You've got egg on your chin."

He wiped it away. "Good?"

"Yep."

The doors buzzed and a green light flicked on. Brandon pulled a door open, and they entered a nicely carpeted interior hallway with amber-colored lights along the walls, which featured a large mural of downtown Portland.

A door opened ahead on the left and a tall, blond woman stepped out, nodded in silence, and motioned for them to come in.

Of course, Deetz kept things light with a happy good morning and introductions, while Brandon walked into the lavish condo with his mouth hanging open. The view of the river and city skyline through floor-to-ceiling tinted windows was breathtaking. Everything in the condo was white, silver metal, and glass, from the leather couches and contemporary tables to the thick rugs and streamlined fireplace—which featured a thin line of flames dancing amidst clear glass pebbles.

As Darlene guided them to the sunken central living area, Deetz realized she was rail thin—to the point of looking anorexic. She wore expensive black running pants, a matching top, and bright orange Hoka running shoes. As she sat and motioned for them to do the same, she said nothing about the spread on the glass table, which included a smorgasbord of pastries and fruits.

She quietly asked if they would like coffee or something else to drink and they both declined. Brandon did, however, help himself to the largest danish in the basket, for which Deetz shot him a questioning glance.

Deetz made small talk about working with Brandon and asked if Darlene had any children.

"Uh, no, Chris can't . . . we can't have children."

After recovering from that awkward moment, Deetz explained that they were investigating the Greg Newman shootings at the offices of Jumpy Jim's Coffee, and that Brandon would be recording the conversation. She popped up, excused herself, told Alexa to turn up the heat, and grabbed a gray fleece jacket that was draped over a barstool.

"I must say, I was surprised you wanted to speak to me," Darlene said ever so softly as she wrapped the jacket around her shoulders and sat back down on the loveseat adjacent to the couch where Deetz and Brandon were sitting.

As Deetz lied slightly that their visit was somewhat of a formality, he stumbled a bit as he got a better look at Darlene Dowdy's face. Her small, glassy brown eyes were sunk deep in her skull and were surrounded above and below by thick, exaggerated swollen patches. Her small nose was red, her cracked lips full of Botox, her cheeks hollow, and her neck slender and fragile. Any bruising wouldn't be visible because she was so bundled up.

"Why don't we just start with what you know about your husband's relationship with Gregory Newman?" Deetz said.

Darlene wrapped tighter in the jacket and squinted. "See, that's what I mean. Shouldn't you be asking my husband about that? Again, I'm kind of confused why I'm being questioned?"

"Well, Mrs. Dowdy—"

"And, by the way, my husband wasn't happy about this. He sees no reason I should be questioned. He said you cancelled your appointment with him."

"We will be talking to him. Mrs. Dowdy, it's our job to make sure Gregory Newman acted alone, and that there are no other . . . leads we need to pursue," Deetz said. "So, to that end, can you please tell us what you know about Chris's relationship with Greg Newman?"

She scowled and shook her head. "I stay out of company business so I'm not going to be a big help."

"Did Chris say anything about Greg Newman leading up to when he got fired last Friday, or leading up to the shooting Monday?"

She made a sour face. "No. I barely even heard the . . . his name before the shooting."

"So, you're not aware of any attempt your husband may've made to have Greg Newman use company funds to pay-off his gambling debts?"

"Pfft. No. It wouldn't surprise me, but again, he wouldn't tell me. We just don't have that kind of relationship."

"Does Chris have gambling debts?" Deetz said.

Her eyebrows shot up and she gave a slight chuckle. "I honestly don't keep track of his gambling. His hobbies are his hobbies, not mine. I mean, I know he bets. I don't know if he wins or loses. I know his dad's been furious with him before, about his betting—about a lot of things."

Deetz glanced at Brandon, who was wide-eyed.

Several fragrant candles burned and flickered on the mantel, giving off a heavy pine scent that was bothering Deetz's eyes.

"In our investigation, Mrs. Dowdy, unfortunately accusations have been made about your husband . . . having or attempting to have sexual relations with other women—sometimes under duress. Can you—"

"Stop!" Darlene cursed and stood up.

"I'm sorry, Mrs. Dowdy, we've come upon some serious allegations pertaining to your husband. One involves drug-rape and the other sexual harassment."

Darlene crossed her arms and walked to the vast windows. She peered out with her back to the officers.

"Mrs. Dowdy, were you aware Chris had an affair with Greg Newman's wife?"

Darlene stood still and said nothing. There was a full-blown glass-and-mirror bar to her right and Deetz half wondered if she might just pour herself a tall glass of bourbon and throw it back.

"Are the names Jackie Brooks or Carrie Sandowski familiar to you?" Deetz continued, awkwardly.

Slowly, Darlene turned, walked to the bar, opened a white glass box, and took out a pack of cigarettes and a lighter. She knocked one out of the pack and stuck the long white cigarette in the corner of her mouth, lit it, and put the items back in the box. She glanced at the officers, exhaled through her nose, walked back over to where she'd been standing, and pulled open one of the heavy sliding glass doors, which took every ounce of energy in her one hundred pound body.

"I honestly don't have anything to say to you," she finally said, standing with one foot inside the condo and one on the spacious balcony. "I'm sorry you wasted your time."

Brandon looked at Deetz questioningly.

Deetz had one last thing he could try. "Mrs. Dowdy, we know Family Services was here in December—on a domestic violence call."

He didn't plan on mentioning Tammy, of course.

Darlene leaned against the glass, tilted her head back, and blew a tight stream of blue smoke out the door; the smoke whipped away in the May wind.

Deetz stood. He motioned for Brandon to stay seated and he walked to within five feet of Darlene Dowdy.

"Ma'am, I've been doing this a long time; almost thirty-five years," Deetz said evenly. "Something in my gut told me we needed to talk to you today. And I think I was right. I can tell something is very wrong. Please, let us—"

"How dare you!" She fired the cigarette across the balcony and stomped inside. "You don't know anything about me!"

"I know you called Family Services and that your neck and arms were bruised, and one of these sliding doors was cracked, and the place was a mess. There'd been a fight. He'd hurt you."

Her mouth curled into an angry frown, and she inhaled deeply through her nose as she set her slender shoulders back. "Don't do this." She sniffed and shook her head. "Don't come in here like Superman thinking you can solve all my problems and then just leave." She laughed and cried at the same time. "You can't help me. No one can."

"Mrs. Dowdy, you didn't fall down the steps that night. Your life was in danger. If your husband is hurting you, hurting other women, he needs to be stopped."

She pointed across the room at Brandon. "Turn that recorder off."

Brandon looked at Deetz, who nodded.

Brandon tapped the screen. "It's off," he said.

"I hope you do get him. I hope you find evidence about those other women. I hope you find out he was doing something illegal," she said. "But I can't have anything to do with his demise. I think you understand what I'm saying."

As if on cue, her phone buzzed from the bar.

She looked at Deetz, then Brandon, then marched over and picked it up. She looked at it for a moment, then held the glowing screen out for them to see. She nodded and spoke like a crazy woman. "You see that? That's him. He wants to know if you're gone yet."

She laughed crazily, set the fleece jacket on a barstool, looked at the phone, and read the text message aloud: "'Is he gone? Anyone with him?'" She looked up at them with madness in her eyes, then back at the phone. "'I need names. Write down everything he asked you. I need to know everything.'"

She taps a message into the phone. "Of course, I have to answer him on the spot. Want to know what I wrote back?"

Deetz and Brandon were silent, their mouths and eyes wide open.

She looked at her phone and read aloud what she'd written back to her husband. "'Deetz and cop son here. Leaving now. I'll write down what they asked.'"

She tossed the phone clacking back onto the bar and headed for the front door. "I'm afraid our time's up, officers."

Deetz and Brandon followed her.

She opened the door and stood silent with it open, not making eye contact, looking down and about nervously.

They nodded and walked past her into the hallway.

Deetz turned to make one final plea, but the door was closing.

At the last second, the door stopped and she peered out from a small gap. "I wish I could have said more," Darlene whispered. "I can't. You know why. You're right about everything. I just . . . I can't be the one to tell."

The door clicked shut.

Then locked.

## 25

J.P. SIPPED A FRESHLY ground cup of Jumpy Jim's coffee in his small office on the fourth floor of the Farris-Junger Office Complex and realized he shouldn't have come in at all. It was almost 11 a.m. and his skull was pounding beneath the gauze and bandages.

Employees had been sent home Monday and Tuesday and were given the option to work remotely the remainder of the week. There were probably only twelve to fifteen people working somberly throughout the spacious, low-lit fourth floor: definitely a skeleton crew.

Tammy had urged J.P. to stay home, rest, and do a little work from his place, but he'd already missed three days and had several important events coming up that he needed to work on, plus he had more than two hundred emails to sort through.

Christopher Dowdy was in his office with his father and the door was closed, but J.P. had heard them talking loudly earlier, including some yelling. He planned on avoiding Dowdy at all costs, especially because he knew Christopher would have found out by now that Deetz and Brandon had interviewed his wife earlier that morning.

There was a tap at J.P.'s door and Kyle Ford leaned around the doorframe and stuck his head in. "You got a minute?"

Kyle had worked alongside Gregory Newman and was now filling in as interim controller.

"Sure. Come in," J.P. said.

"How's the head?" said Kyle, a tall, thin guy with shiny black hair combed straight back with styling gel, a slender face, a smattering of freckles, and blue eyes.

"Not so great," J.P. said. "I'm going to get out of here in a little while." He sipped his coffee and set the cup on his desk.

"Sounds like a good idea. Listen," Kyle paused and looked around to make sure no one was within earshot, "how much do you know about our arrangement with Laser Direct?"

"Oh man, here we go. What now?"

Kyle again looked out for anyone nearby then pulled a chair close to J.P. and sat on the edge of it. "A payment was made to them recently for a hundred and fifty grand," he whispered. "Above and beyond their normal monthly fee."

"What day? Who did it?" J.P.'s face burned.

"Last Thursday. The old man. He went right over me. I'm worried, dude. We're not going to last if this kind of crazy stuff keeps happening."

Shouting suddenly came from Christopher Dowdy's office, but it was unintelligible.

J.P. and Kyle looked at each other.

"They've been doing that on and off all morning," J.P. said.

"Yeah, I heard the old man call Dowdy a screw up. He said he was tired of covering up his tracks for him. I mean he sounded furious."

"Greg had suspicions about Laser Direct, you know that."

Kyle nodded. "He said we wouldn't make it to Thanksgiving under Dowdy's leadership. He was sure he was stealing from the company. He was trying to prove it."

J.P. leaned back in his swivel chair, took a deep breath, and exhaled. He locked his fingers behind his head and swiveled. This was confirmation he needed to get out of Jumpy Jim's as fast as possible. And he wasn't about to try to be a hero and somehow bring the Dowdys to justice. Christopher Dowdy was a psycho and J.P. wanted to get as far away from him as he possibly could.

"What do we do about this payment?" Kyle said. "This is part of why Greg was so messed up. Do we take it to the board—over Dowdy's head? We're in a bad downward spiral, J.P."

J.P. wasn't going to tell Kyle he was planning to leave the company.

"Greg had a theory that the people at Laser Direct were actually hired by the Dowdys—really that it was their company," Kyle whispered. "He believed they use a bare minimum team, charge us a ton, and keep truckloads of the fees for themselves. It sounds far-fetched but now I wonder. And what about this payment—a hundred and fifty grand? We should have listened to Greg."

"Look man," J.P. leaned forward and rested his elbows on his knees. "When it comes right down to it, this is between Dowdy and Will Tomason. They own the dang company. The board needs to do something."

"Should I go to Tomason?" Kyle said.

J.P. closed his eyes and thought how hopeless it was. Jumpy Jim's was a fast-sinking ship. He'd lost his love for the company the day Dowdy came in and poisoned everything.

J.P. eyed Kyle, trying to figure out how to say it. "I think, at this point, everybody needs to do some soul searching. I know I am."

Kyle leaned back and tilted his head with a look of surprise. "Oh wow. I never thought you'd leave. Everyone's leaving. You can't, man. We can't lose you."

"I didn't say I was leaving."

"I can tell."

"It's not the same company it was when it started."

"I can't lose this job, man. We just bought a house." Kyle's eyes were huge and glassy with tears and his face had turned red.

J.P. felt for him. "If I were you, dude, I'd do two things—tell Tomason about the payout today and forget about it, it's out of your hands; he needs to go to the board. Second, start getting your resumé out, like today."

Kyle stood in frustration, hands on his waist, and paced, muttering about how they'd just closed on the house ten days ago.

"That's enough!" The words thundered from Christopher Dowdy's office, words yelled by his father, Alexander.

Then the door to Dowdy's office swung open and banged the wall.

Alexander Dowdy stepped out red-faced, then turned back and

said something more to his son, jabbing a finger at him. All J.P. could make out were the words, "make it fast."

Then Alexander Dowdy turned back and his angry eyes settled on J.P. and Kyle from across the maze of cubicles.

"What the heck," Kyle whispered.

Alexander raised a hand as if wanting their attention, then headed toward them.

"He's coming here. I'm gone, man." Kyle ducked out and headed in the opposite direction.

J.P. stood and watched Alexander weave his way toward him. The man was broad-shouldered, about six-foot-three, tan, full head of black and gray hair, fine navy suit, with leather suspenders and matching wingtips.

J.P. turned and walked back into his office. Paperwork covered his desk. His head ached. He still had lots of work to do, but knew he needed to go home and rest. The doctors had told him not to overdo it.

J.P. caught a huge whiff of Alexander's cologne and the man's large frame filled the doorway. "You got a couple minutes?" He looked at his big, silver watch. "Won't take long. I've got to be somewhere."

"Yeah," J.P. said, his heart racing. "Come in."

"Let's do the terrace . . . do you mind?"

"Uh, yeah, what's it about? I mean, do I need to bring anything?"

"No. I'll see you out there in five. I've got to make a call and hit the head on the way."

"Okay."

Alexander smacked the doorframe and left.

J.P. walked over to his window and looked out at the city streets below. An eerie feeling came over him. He didn't usually deal with Alexander, had only talked to the man a handful of times, and considered him cold and inward-focused—the type who looked over your shoulder when he was talking to you. Since J.P. was over public relations and Alexander dealt more in overall operations, their paths rarely crossed.

J.P. walked back over to his door and looked across to Christopher Dowdy's office. His door was closed.

*Something's goin' on . . . something not good.*

J.P. walked to his desk, retrieved three extra-strength Tylenol, and threw them back with a swig from his lukewarm coffee. Then he grabbed his coat from the back of a chair and put it on. He walked back to the window, got his phone out, went to his Notes, and found the one he'd typed in the morning before. He read it silently. "Peace I leave with you; my peace I give to you. I do not give to you as the world gives. Do not let your hearts be troubled and do not be afraid."

He closed his eyes.

*Be with me.*

Then he looked back down at the phone, opened the recorder app, touched the red button to start recording, dropped the phone in the breast pocket of his jacket, and headed for the terrace.


IT WAS ALWAYS dark in the part of the offices back by the copy machines, water cooler, and espresso machine. J.P. made his way around the yellow police tape that still blocked off where the Greg Newman shooting took place. He said hello to Jill Guest, who stopped to ask how he was doing while she quietly made copies.

A weird and solemn vibe hung over the place.

He got to the door to the terrace and looked out. Alexander wasn't out there yet, but J.P. zipped up his coat and went out anyway. The sun was peeking through off-and-on amid fast-moving clouds and gusty winds. It felt good.

The terrace—about forty feet wide and twenty feet deep—featured several tables with closed umbrellas, chairs, and benches.

J.P. walked to the far railing and glanced down at the city from the fourth floor. The leaves on the trees were starting to come out and he looked forward to summer. He thought of Tammy and how he'd planned to propose to her in May or June, but now that would be on hold until he found another job.

He heard the door open and turned to face Alexander Dowdy, whose coat whipped in the wind as he walked out.

"Oh crap, I didn't realize it was so windy. Come over here." He walked to a bench against the concrete wall but did not sit. "I can't believe they haven't gotten rid of all that police crap yet. That should be long gone, it's been four days. Maybe your cop family can do something about that for us."

It had really only been three days. J.P. walked over and stood facing him, not liking how this was starting out.

"So your dad and brother interviewed Christopher's wife this morning," Alexander said, brushing his sleeves.

"Oh? I don't know about that."

"Oh, you don't?" Alexander said sarcastically. "They asked her about Christopher's relationship with that maniac Newman."

*Huh uh, not going there.*

"Okay . . . so what did you want to meet about?" J.P. thought of the scripture, about keeping it peaceful.

Alexander tilted his head and squinted at J.P. "Where would they've gotten the idea Christopher had gambling debts? Hmm? Did you tell them that?"

J.P. was taken aback.

Alarms carved out his insides with a sickening feeling.

Was this grown man about to attack him?

Alexander had to be sixty-five, but he was strong, huge hands.

*Is this why he wanted to meet out here, to fight?*

"I don't have anything to do with their investigation." J.P. felt lightheaded.

The two men stared at each other with tension sizzling between them. Alexander was a good six inches taller than J.P.

"What're they doing, exactly? Why are they coming after Christopher—and me for that matter?"

"Look, if this doesn't pertain to business, I'm heading back in." J.P. turned to leave.

"Hold it. Hold it, Deetz."

J.P. turned back and they glared at each other.

"I'm just trying to figure out why they're trying to turn a routine office shooting into a witch hunt for my son?"

"Again, that's not my business—"

"Oh, *it is* your business because your last name is Deetz and you work under my son, and me for that matter. So not only do we have you and your brother and your dad involved, we've got your girl-friend involved, too."

*Oh no you didn't.*

This was getting way too weird.

"I don't know what you're talking about."

"Oh you don't?" Alexander stepped closer to J.P. "What about domestic violence? Now do you know what I'm talking about? Tammy does."

"Leave Tammy out of this!" J.P. said and braced his legs. He wasn't backing up a step further. He would fight the guy if he had to.

"Leave *Christopher* out of this, and me—or else!"

"Or else?" J.P. said exaggeratedly. "Is that what you just said?"

Thoughts spun through J.P.'s mind—he hoped the recorder was getting everything, he and his family were being threatened, the whole thing was surreal.

Alexander's mouth sealed closed and he set his shoulders back and surveyed J.P.

"You need to call off your family and you need to do it now," Alexander said.

J.P. laughed innocently. "I have nothing to do with their police work. Besides, if Chris and you are innocent, what's there to worry about? They're simply making sure Newman acted alone."

"Christopher has had issues, okay?" Alexander spit out a slew of expletives. "He'd be the first to admit he's got . . . problems. That's part of the reason I came in, to help steady the ship."

"I really don't want to talk about this."

Alexander lowered his head and pinched the bridge of his nose. A gust of wind whipped and the sun came out bright.

Alexander clenched his teeth, leaned closer, and said, "I don't trust you, Deetz."

"Why don't we talk about the business? Why don't we talk about the hundred-fifty thousand dollars that went to Laser Direct a week ago?"

"That little . . ." Alexander cussed and stomped away from J.P., then spun around to face him from ten feet away. "Do you know how many businesses I've started? How many corporations I've turned around, taken from worst to first? What am I even saying? I don't need to explain myself to a simpleton peon who doesn't know his—"

"Shut up, man!" J.P.'s heart thundered and his head pounded.

"I'm not doing this with you. If you want to talk about my job and work, fine. Otherwise, leave me alone."

Alexander stalked toward J.P. with a long index finger pointed at him.

"Don't you talk to me like that, *punk*. I'll bash your skull in. And then I'll fire you."

"Oh, that would really make things better for your little Christopher, wouldn't it?"

Alexander stopped in his tracks four feet from J.P.

His tan face morphed into that of a dragon.

"You better call off your father and brother right now, you get me? You drag my name through the mud and I'll sue your family for every last cent—along with the Portland Police Bureau." He walked right up to J.P., leaned within twelve inches of his face, and said quietly. "Besides that, we wouldn't want anything to happen to dear Tammy now, would we?"

He shoved J.P. as he stalked past him, threw the door open, and disappeared inside.

**26**

———————

Deetz and Brandon picked up burgers and fries from Jack in the Box and headed to J.P.'s apartment at 1:15 p.m. to meet J.P. and listen to the recording of his confrontation with Alexander Dowdy. Deetz was surprised when Tammy answered the door and helped them bring the bags in; she'd taken a late lunch from work and had run over to see how J.P. was doing.

"We'd have brought you lunch if we knew you were going to be here, Tammy," Deetz said. "How about we cut my burger in half, I honestly won't eat it all anyway."

Tammy politely turned him down insisting she'd been looking forward to leftover sloppy joes, which her mom had made for J.P. the evening before.

Deetz wasn't going to say anything as he sat down, but J.P. didn't look well. He was lying on the couch in jeans, a black V-neck sweater, and moccasins—and his face was pasty. Half circles below his eyes were slightly purple, the same color as his lips.

"Dude, you look like death." Brandon went ahead and said it as he unwrapped his burger. "Are you sure you don't have an infection or something?"

"Overdid it," J.P. said, gently touching the bandages on his head.

"I told him not to go in," Tammy yelled from the kitchen. "Drink the Gatorade, J.P."

J.P. reached over to the table, grabbed a big silver thermal cup,

135

and sipped from the straw. Then he grunted as he sat up and leaned over the coffee table where they'd spread out the food. "I'm starved."

Brandon got two bottled waters for him and his dad, and they gathered around the coffee table and began to eat.

"Well, let's hear this infamous recording," Brandon said, motioning toward J.P.'s phone.

J.P. scowled and put a finger to his lips. "Shhh. I don't want her to hear it."

Deetz shot him a puzzled look and Brandon threw his hands up and whispered, "That's why we're here."

"He mentions Tammy!" J.P. whispered angrily. "I didn't know she was going to be here."

"Did I hear my name?" Tammy called from the kitchen.

A second later she entered the room and stopped hesitantly with a smile, holding a plate and a bottled water. "What's going on?"

Deetz raised his eyebrows awkwardly and so did Brandon. They both looked at J.P. for a response.

"Nothing, nothing. All good. Not having a bun?"

"What're you guys doing?" Tammy walked over and sat down next to J.P., put her plate down, and spread out a napkin. "What did I hear you say about a recording?"

The guys all looked at each other and were speechless.

"Oh boy." Tammy looked at each one of them, her smile turning into a frown. "What have I walked into?"

Finally, J.P. spoke up. "Okay. Christopher Dowdy's dad said he wanted to talk to me this morning. I didn't have a good feeling about it, so I recorded it."

Tammy's body tensed and her pretty brown eyes bore into J.P. like lasers, then she looked at the others. "That's why you guys are here?" She shook her head and readjusted her napkin. "I thought it was just a social call."

The men were silent and the air was filled with uncertainty.

"Well, go ahead, play it," Tammy said, taking a bite of a carrot. "I'm a big girl."

J.P. cleared his throat. "Honey, the thing is, he mentioned you."

They stared at each other and Tammy stopped chewing.

"He brought up when you went to Dowdy's place on the domestic violence call," J.P. said.

"His *dad* brought that up?" Tammy said.

"Yeah. I don't want you to hear it, okay? I just don't. It's nothing terrible. It's just . . . you don't need to be bothered with it."

"Fine, that's fine." Tammy stood and grabbed her plate and water.

"Sorry, Tammy," Deetz said.

"It's fine. I get it. Official police business." She walked into the kitchen and the guys looked at each other.

"You can eat in my room if you want," J.P. called. "It's probably too cold on the balcony."

Tammy came back into the living room with her coat on, holding her water. "I'm just gonna head back to the office. I've got a lot going on today," she said. "It's good to see you guys. J.P., you look awful and you need to sleep and drink that Gatorade. Okay, I'm out."


WHEN DEETZ, Brandon, and J.P. finished listening to the recording of J.P.'s argument with Alexander Dowdy, Brandon was visibly livid. Deetz felt the same but covered it well.

"What a pompous jerk!" Brandon said. "We need to arrest him. Dad, can we do that? He threatened Tammy, and all of us."

"Two problems," Deetz said. "Number one, it's a veiled threat. Not enough upon which to build a case—"

"Dad, come on!" Brandon said. "Bash your skull in? Fire you?"

Deetz held up a hand for Brandon to cool down.

"Okay, let's say the threat is strong enough. The problem is, legally, the recording isn't admissible because J.P. didn't have Alexander's permission to record."

"You've got to be kidding," J.P. said. "Are you sure? They do it on shows all the time."

Deetz nodded. "Clear this stuff off." He started putting their trash in the bags, cleared a space, and got his pad and pen. "I've done this in my head a million times, but we need to make a list of Christopher and Alexander Dowdy's illegal and non-illegal activities."

Brandon and J.P. emptied the coffee table and threw the trash away in the kitchen, then returned for the powwow with their dad.

Ten minutes later—after an in-depth discussion—Deetz's pad contained the following scribblings:

Illegal:
~ Dowdys threatened Greg Newman (pretending to be Mob) to pay gambling debts w/ company funds
~ Used company funds to pay dad (embezzlement)
~ Possible money laundering or embezzlement via Laser Direct
~ Chris drug-raped Jackie Brooks (no evidence, just her testimony)
~ Chris threatened Carrie Sandowski for sex (no evidence, just secondhand testimony from Jackie Brooks)
~ Alexander threatened J.P./Tammy to get police off case

Non-illegal:
~ Chris had affair with Greg Newman's wife (Jessica)
~ Chris came onto Tammy at domestic violence call
~ Chris had affairs with others

Deetz tossed the pad onto the table. J.P. picked it up, looked it over, and handed it to Brandon.

"I want to question Alexander Dowdy next," Deetz said.

"We can't arrest either of them?" Brandon said.

"It's too thin, son. We're getting there," Deetz said. "We need evidence. We need to drill down into Laser Direct. I'd like to find a trail for the fictitious Mob threat toward Greg Newman."

"But even if we can just find proof the Dowdys have taken money illegally from Jumpy Jim's, that'll be good enough, right?" Brandon said.

Deetz nodded hesitantly. "Yeah, but I want to find everything."

"So what's next?" J.P. said.

"Right now I'm going to call Tidwell and get warrants to confiscate the Dowdys' phones, laptops, desktops, and corporate records. After we review all that, we'll bring Alexander in for questioning."

"They're gonna be furious," J.P. said.

"Tough," Brandon said.

"I'm just saying, I've got to work there," J.P. said.

"Stay away from them. Keep your distance," Deetz said. "Tomorrow's Friday. You need to be out sick, make it a three-day weekend. By Monday things will have cooled down."

"Seriously dude. You need to rest," Brandon said.

Deetz's phone vibrated. He looked. It was Joanie calling.

"It's your mother," Deetz said. "Hey, babe, I'm just sitting here with your two handsome sons—"

"Are you still at J.P.'s?" Joanie said, abruptly.

"Yeah, what's up?"

"Turn on KOIN news. Hurry."

## 27

Brandon, Deetz, and J.P. stood in front of the TV while J.P. fiddled with the remote until he found KOIN news. "Here it is," he said.

A red, white, and blue Breaking News banner scrolled across the top of the screen. Beneath it stood the same female reporter Brandon had made the mistake of blabbing to at the Newman residence several days earlier.

"Oh no," Brandon said. "Amanda Kim—"

"Shh," Deetz hissed.

"Once again," Amanda said, "we are *live* just outside the gates of the Flint Hill Memorial Gardens in Vermont Hills where the body of the shooter from Monday's massacre at the offices of Jumpy Jim's Coffee, Gregory Newman, is being laid to rest."

"What are they doing there?" Brandon said. "Ridiculous—"

"Would you shut up?" J.P. said.

The camera panned from the huge, arching iron gates of the cemetery, across the street to a cluster of some twenty-five people, many of whom appeared to be media—juggling cameras, lights, and microphones.

"In a rather unprecedented series of events," Amanda continued, "Christopher Dowdy, one of the owners of Jumpy Jim's Coffee, and his father Alexander Dowdy, who serves as a consultant for the company, have announced they will be having an impromptu press conference here in just a few moments."

"What?" Brandon said. "What now?"

J.P.'s face was pale. He sat down on the coffee table.

"As you can see on your screen now . . . are we cutting to the drone? Yes, here it is . . ."

The image on the screen flicked to a hovering overhead shot of the cemetery and a large blue tent, surrounded by headstones, green grass, and a black cinder driveway.

"What you're seeing from our incredible KOIN news drone is the burial site where Gregory Newman is being laid to rest and, from what we understand, there is a very small graveside service happening right now—beneath that blue tent. We know Newman's wife Jessica is present, along with their three young children, and we believe several relatives may be in attendance, but that's about it."

The crystal-clear footage from the drone slowly panned in a circular motion around the tent and then suddenly backed away, high up into the sky, revealing more and more of the vast cemetery grounds, the gated entrance, and the group of people gathered across the street.

"We've also learned that a local priest, Father Clancy Byrne, who did not previously know the family, is giving a brief eulogy, or, should I say, final sentiments. We understand this is the only service there has been for Newman, the thirty-three-year-old former controller of Jumpy Jim's, who opened fire at the company's fourth floor headquarters in the Farris-Junger Office Complex downtown this past Monday. As you know, three people were wounded in the attack and three people died, including Newman, who was shot by Portland Police."

Deetz and J.P. both looked at Brandon for any reaction, but he just stood there staring solemnly at the TV.

Amanda Kim appeared again, her eyes darting about as she pressed two fingers against her right ear. "Okay, wow, I'm being told right now that the Dowdys are not going to wait until this service for Gregory Newman has ended. They are going to start their press conference right now. So, we are sending you over, across the street. Again, this will be the CEO of Jumpy Jim's Coffee,

Christopher Dowdy, and his father and company consultant, Alexander Dowdy."

Even though Christopher was the bigwig CEO, the scene showing him and his dad, surrounded by reporters and microphones, looked as if his father was the one in command. Alexander Dowdy stood tall with his broad shoulders back and his tan face held high, jaw clenched, examining each face in the crowd. While he wore a navy suit, yellow tie, and suspenders, Christopher was dressed down in a gray Nike windbreaker, black sweatpants, and the trademark silver Bluetooth earpiece sticking out of one ear.

Someone in the crowd said something and both Dowdys leaned toward the voice with eyebrows raised. Then Alexander nodded at Christopher with a scowl, patted his back, and moved him toward a small wooden podium packed with microphones and tape recorders.

Holding a small piece of paper in one hand, Christopher adjusted the main mic, looked left and right, and finally spoke. "Afternoon. As you know, this past Monday we experienced a horrific tragedy at our . . . at the offices of Jumpy Jim's Coffee downtown. The shooter, whose name I'm not going to give the honor of mentioning, is being buried here in Vermont Hills today. To that we say, good riddance."

Christopher paused, looked down at the piece of paper, and began reading directly from it. "Even though we lost a beloved employee and one of Portland's finest that day—and three other people were wounded—somehow, the ensuing investigation has turned into a witch hunt for the Dowdy family—namely me and my father." Christopher glanced back and waved a hand toward his dad who stood erect, large hands clasped in front of him, dark eyes scanning the crowd.

Christopher cleared his throat and continued. "We called this press conference to get way out in front of any rumors, lies, or inuendo that the public may hear coming out of the Portland Police Bureau. What happened at our offices Monday was nothing more and nothing less than the actions of a mentally ill individual, a coward who was most likely upset about being let go the previous week—"

Reporters' frenzied questions interrupted Dowdy.

"What did he do wrong?"

"Why was he fired?"

"Who fired him and why?"

"Was there any warning?"

Christopher's confused face cranked from one reporter to the next; he was obviously taken aback by the barrage of questions.

Alexander Dowdy suddenly shook his head vehemently, wagged a long finger at the reporters, and stepped right up to the mic, nudging Christopher to one side.

"Hold it, hold it, hold it. That is uncalled for." Alexander adjusted the mic clumsily and bent over it, his low voice booming. "Have some manners. We weren't finished with our statement." He leaned way back, inhaled deeply, sighed, and bent back over the mic. "This is a warning—to the Portland Police Bureau. Don't you dare try to turn Monday's tragedy into anything more than it was— a senseless act by a deranged coward."

Christopher Dowdy stood off to the side sheepishly, like a child who'd just butchered his piano recital. Alexander didn't even look at him.

"Our employees have been interrogated, even our family members . . . it's absolutely ludicrous. Have some common sense. Have some common decency," Alexander continued. "And there's one more very important piece of this thing we want to bring to light today."

"This guy's a royal jerk," Brandon said.

"I can't argue with you there," Deetz said.

"I don't like where this is heading," J.P. said.

Alexander rubbed his jaw with a big hand and paused at length, seemingly for dramatic affect. Meanwhile, camera motor drives fired away like the paparazzi and reporters shouted questions. Alexander shook his head with a slight grin and wagged a finger at the reporters. Then he leaned back down over the mic and spoke in a low, booming voice.

"Does anyone find it interesting that the two Portland Police officers putting all the heat on my son and me—Investigator Wayne Deetz and his rookie cop son Brandon Deetz—are *related* to one of our employees at Jumpy Jim's?"

A wave of murmurs rolled through the crowd.

"I thought you'd find that interesting." Alexander raised his voice above the commotion. "J.P. Deetz is our very own director of public relations. In fact, he and my son Christopher hid in a conference room together in the Jumpy Jim's offices when Gregory Newman was on his rampage."

J.P.'s mouth dropped open and his eyes doubled in size as he looked at Deetz and Brandon, then back at the TV.

Reporters pushed toward Alexander, yelling questions.

"Quiet. Quiet right now!" he demanded. "If there are any questions remaining unanswered in this tragedy, the one glaring one is this: why did J.P. Deetz do nothing to protect the employees of Jumpy Jim's when *he knew ahead of time* that Gregory Newman had threatened to shoot up the office?"

"What?" J.P. jumped to his feet.

Brandon cursed and Deetz hushed them both.

The camera jiggled from all the movement in the crowd.

"If you will use some manners and let me finish." Alexander held up both hands to silence everyone and adjusted the mic. "All we know is that, while Christopher and J.P. Deetz were in hiding, Deetz made a regretful comment that he should have done something, because Gregory Newman had warned him that he was going to, quote-unquote, 'shoot up the place.'"

The reporters went crazy.

"That is not true, Dad!" J.P. yelled. "Greg never said that. *I* never said that!"

Deetz put a finger to his lips so they could hear the rest.

Brandon was so mad his face was on fire.

"Perhaps Portland Police—someone other than J.P. Deetz's father and brother—can focus on this glaring question of why nothing was done when the shooter gave fair warning about his intentions."

"That lying—"

"Shh," Deetz hissed.

Alexander stretched out a long arm and brought his son close to him. "That is all we have today. We are not going to take questions at this time because what we just told you is all we know about this matter."

---

## 28

FRIDAY MORNING WAS BITING cold with wind and rain. Brandon felt as numb and dismal as the weather. With the four-days-on, three-days-off schedule, he and Deetz were supposed to be off duty that day, but the Dowdy press conference the afternoon before had sparked a firestorm of national press coverage which Sergeant Tidwell insisted demanded a unified response from the Portland Police Bureau.

Wearing their heavy navy police rain parkas and hats, and black mourning bands on their arms, Brandon and Deetz stood next to each other—alongside Virgil Bennett and Sid Sikorski—atop the front steps of police headquarters. Tidwell was stationed at a podium in front of them addressing dozens of reporters, most of whom stood and squatted beneath umbrellas at the bottom of the steps.

"We are about to lay to rest one of Portland's finest and bravest, officer Danny Rodriguez." Tidwell's deep voice sounded almost omniscient in the dark morning rain. "All alone, Danny entered the offices of Jumpy Jim's Coffee this past Monday morning with one purpose and that was to stop a crazed gunman. By God's grace he was able to wound the offender, which ultimately led to his capture and death."

Brandon was depressed and outraged. And he was sick to his

stomach over the violence and evil and lies he'd experienced in less than a week on the job.

Danny's widow Renee stood in a daze under cover off to the side with the couple's two young girls, both wearing shiny pink raincoats and shivering with their mom's gloved hands on their shoulders. An eight-by-ten framed photo of Danny in uniform, encircled by a wreath, sat alone on a pedestal next to them.

Some twenty squad cars and a dozen horses with steam puffing from their wet noses lined SW 2nd Avenue for the upcoming procession. Danny's cruiser—number 0028—was parked at an angle to the right of the steps where mourners had piled it with an array of flowers eight inches thick.

Tidwell told the crowd that Danny dreamed of being a police officer ever since he was a boy growing up in Oakland, California. He said Danny loved gardening, walks with his wife, making lasagna, dates with his girls, and bowling in the police league on Thursday nights; he averaged one-fifty-two and once rolled a league-high two-thirty-eight.

"Before we begin the procession over to St. Patrick's and Peace Gardens, let me briefly address the press conference held yesterday by Christopher and Alexander Dowdy, who work at Jumpy Jim's Coffee." Tidwell shuffled his notes and took a moment to review them and compose himself. "Investigator Wayne Deetz standing back here to my right, has been with the PPB for thirty-five years. The only reason he's in uniform is because he's riding with his son Brandon, also behind me, as Brandon does his field training. I asked investigator Deetz to take on the investigation of the Jumpy Jim's shooting because he is a consummate professional and because his other adult son, J.P., was in the offices at the time of the event—an employee of Jumpy Jim's.

"Our goal in this investigation is to determine whether the shooter acted alone and, if possible, to uncover a motive for the shooting," Tidwell continued. "We also want to make sure there was no illegal activity or any underlying tension that may have brought on this tragic incident."

When Tidwell paused, reporters began barking questions, but he simply raised his voice and continued. "As the head of this department, I am completely satisfied with how the investigation has unfolded thus far and I am one hundred percent confident with the team we have in place. We don't expect it to go on much longer. And, of course, we are interviewing many people to make sure we do the most thorough job possible to get to the truth—"

"Did the shooter warn J.P. Deetz he was going to shoot up the office?" a male reporter yelled at the top of his lungs. All the other reporters kept quiet because they wanted to know the same thing.

Tidwell tilted his head and gave the guy a disgusted look that chastised him without a word. "I'm not going to address that because this is a live, ongoing investigation," Tidwell said, "but I can assure you every single lead is being followed, we're going by the book, and we're going to find out exactly what happened in this terrible event. Now, if we may, let's turn the focus back to what we're here for, and that's to honor the life of a true hero . . ."

ON THE WAY to their patrol cars to get in line for the procession, Tidwell called out to Deetz and Brandon. The rain had turned to drizzle. The wind whipped.

"Good job, Sarge," Deetz said as he and Brandon squared up with Tidwell, Sid, and Virgil at Tidwell's Interceptor.

Brandon rubbed his hands and blew into them for warmth.

"Wayne," Tidwell said, "we need to be absolutely sure J.P. didn't know about any warning from Greg Newman."

They'd already assured everyone of that, and Brandon wondered why he was doubling back on it.

"Sir, the only thing like that said in that conference room when they were hiding was Christopher Dowdy saying he should have killed that twerp when he had the chance," Deetz said. "That was a direct reference to Greg Newman and to the fight they'd had at the park days earlier when Dowdy threw his phone into the river. That's it. J.P. would say if—"

"We need to be positive, that's all I'm saying," Tidwell said bluntly.

*Whoa. He's feeling the pressure from somewhere or someone.*

"To have you and Brandon and J.P. all involved—it does . . . it can look weird," Tidwell said. "That's my fault. I should've thought it through more."

"Sarge, you can count on us," Deetz said.

Brandon nodded as well.

They split up and got into their respective police vehicles.

Brandon buckled up to drive and said, "What was that all about? We'd been through all that."

Deetz strapped in and told Brandon which lights to put on for the procession. Then he said, "I'm not sure. He's under a lot of pressure. I don't feel like he's been himself lately . . . Yeah. I dunno. I'll be glad when this whole thing's over."

Deetz's phone buzzed. He got it out and looked at the screen, then answered. "Hey, Tammy, what's up?" He glanced at Brandon with a look of concern.

Deetz listened. Brandon could hear Tammy's voice but couldn't make out what she was saying.

"What did you do when you saw him?" Deetz said. "Wait, Tammy, Brandon's here. Can I put you on speaker?"

Deetz tapped the speaker button on his phone and caught Brandon up on what was happening. "Christopher Dowdy was standing at his car under an umbrella watching her when she left for work this morning," Deetz said. "Tammy, what'd you do?"

"He wanted to scare me," she said over the speaker. "He was being obvious. I mean, he was staring right at me. He also . . . he had a hand in his coat pocket, as if he had a gun, but I doubt he did. I thought about going back inside, but I've got work to do. I just got in my car and came to my office. He didn't follow me—I don't think. J.P.'s on his way over. I'm fine, but J.P. wanted me to call you."

Brandon fumed and mumbled some choice names for Dowdy.

"I'm sorry that happened, Tammy," Deetz said. "That family has some serious issues. Do you want us to come over?"

"Oh, heavens no," she said. "I'm fine. I told J.P. he didn't have to, but he insisted."

"That's good. I'm glad he is," Deetz said. "If it happens again, I want you to call me immediately. Do you understand?"

**29**

———

J.P.'s heart pounded as he weaved in and out of traffic as fast as he could to get to Tammy's office. The roads were slick, and occasional wind gusts actually shook his car at times.

He couldn't fathom the brazenness of Christopher Dowdy—to stand outside Tammy's apartment! Wait for her to come out! Stand there like he had a gun! Between that and the lies the Dowdys told at the press conference about J.P., he believed they were mentally deranged.

J.P. confirmed with Tammy that Christopher Dowdy was still driving the same car he remembered, a black Cadillac SUV with a matte finish and black wheels; like something out of Chicago P.D.

*Can't miss it.*

On top of everything, J.P. felt like a slug. His head was throbbing and he had zero energy.

"Watch it!" He slammed on his horn as a beat-up blue compact car faded into his lane. At the sound of the horn the car swerved back into its lane. J.P. flew past the car, driven by a girl eating a donut and looking down at her phone.

He glanced in the rearview mirror at his bandages, which looked fine because he'd just changed them that morning. But his pallid face and the dark half-circles beneath his eyes made him look like a prisoner of war.

*Oh well . . . best I can do today.*

He was almost to Tammy's office.

His phone buzzed. He glanced at it. It was Jerome Danson, a purchasing manager and friend from work. J.P. hit speaker and took the call.

"Jerome, what's up?"

"Hey, J.P. You better?" Jerome said.

"Working on it. But yesterday was too soon to go back to work. I'm regretting it."

"Yeah, you probably need to lay low for a while."

The line was silent.

"You still there?" J.P. said, anxious to get to Tammy's office.

"Yeah. Listen, I saw the press conference with Dowdy and his old man yesterday—"

"Jerome, they lied," J.P. said. "Greg Newman did not warn me, I promise you."

"Yeah, that's not why I'm calling. I know your dad's investigating the shooting . . ."

"Yeah?"

"So, something weird happened last week. I haven't said anything to anybody. Maybe I shouldn't. But when I saw the press conference . . . I don't know. Something about the Dowdys is keeping me up at night."

"Join the club. Tell me what weird thing happened."

"Listen, I don't want to be involved or have my name come out in this, okay? This is just something your dad should probably know as he checks everything out."

"Okay, tell me man, because I've got to go in a second." J.P. was only several blocks from the small, house-like office where Tammy worked. It was starting to rain harder.

"Okay, so you know the Indonesian bean supplier that we've argued about in the past—whether we should use their beans, quality issue, blah, blah, blah?"

"Yeah, yeah, yeah. Greg Newman stopped payment to them. That's one of the reasons they fired him. Is that it?"

J.P. approached the driveway for Tammy's office and slowed down.

"Okay, yeah, but here's the tricky thing . . ."

The line went quiet, but J.P. could hear that Jerome was still at the other end. J.P.'s mind was on Tammy as he swung his car into the parking lot of the Family Services Division of the Portland Police Bureau, where Tammy was an investigator. He scanned the lot for Christopher Dowdy's big SUV but didn't see it.

"Jerome, talk to me. I've got to go."

"Everybody probably *thinks* it was Greg Newman's idea to stop that payment—but it wasn't."

J.P. parked abruptly. Turned the car off. Closed his eyes. And focused on what Jerome had just said.

"Alexander Dowdy *told* Greg to stop payment. I heard it," Jerome said. "They had some kind of sick deal going down."

J.P. recoiled. "What?" He looked at Tammy's office and the surrounding area. "Why? How do you know?"

"I worked out on the second floor after work one night last week and I forgot my laptop. When I went up to get it, they were talking on the DL in Christopher's office. Some real serious crap going down."

"Who?"

"The old man and Greg Newman."

J.P. just couldn't get his head around it. "But not Christopher?"

"No, just the two of them—and there's more."

J.P. spotted the matte black Cadillac SUV and his stomach tanked.

It was parked in the empty, crumbling parking lot of the Golden Corral restaurant next-door to Tammy's office.

And it was empty.


J.P. WAS out of his car in a flash.

He would circle the small building first and if he didn't see Dowdy he would go inside.

*God please let Tammy be okay.*

He threw his hood over his head, careful of the bandages.

The rain pelted him.

Cold rainwater seeped into his shoes and socks as he splashed through the mushy grass.

He was light-headed and each hurried step felt oddly off-balance.

If Dowdy had gone inside, J.P. hoped Tammy's colleague Laurice would be in there. He was a giant of a man and didn't take crap from anybody.

J.P. turned the corner at the narrow end of the office.

No one.

This end of the office was closest to Dowdy's car. J.P. examined the vehicle—it was definitely turned off, and empty.

*Hurry.*

He had one more side of the building to find Dowdy and that would be it.

His hood blew off in a gust of wind.

He put it back on as he turned the corner.

Christopher Dowdy stood beneath a black umbrella, wearing black Adidas shorts, a red running jacket, and black socks and shoes.

"Hey!" J.P. yelled. "What do you think you're doing?"

Dowdy chuckled but said nothing.

"What're you doing here?" J.P. slowed as he came within ten feet of the man.

Dowdy swung his shoulders back toward his SUV. This time he wore a big shiny gold Bluetooth device in one ear. "Waitin' for Golden Coral to open. You're getting wet. Where's your umbrella?"

"Look man, I don't know why you're doing what you're doing, but it needs to stop."

"I don't know what you're talking about, J.P. Shouldn't you be at the office? If you're good enough to be running around out here in the rain, you're good enough to be working."

"What are you doing here? What were you doing at Tammy's place this morning?" J.P. was furious and he walked closer to Dowdy. When Dowdy saw that, he squared up with J.P. as if daring him to get physical.

"Answer me!"

Dowdy sneered and that infuriated J.P.

"You stay away from her." He stepped closer to Dowdy and clenched his teeth. "You hear me?"

In a flash, Dowdy swung and slapped J.P.'s head hard with an open hand—right where he'd been shot.

J.P.'s mouth dropped open. He was shocked Dowdy would

purposefully go after his wound. But then again, why be shocked? This family was crazy.

J.P. put his hands up to defend himself but backed up a step.

Dowdy advanced toward him, smirk gone, face serious now.

"Why'd you lie about Greg Newman warning me about the shooting?" J.P. said. "What's that about? Why would you do that unless you're covering something up?"

Dowdy did a shoulder fake and slapped J.P.'s face hard with a left—all while holding his umbrella.

In the next three surreal seconds, J.P. realized he had a decision to make. And what clicked in his mind like the tumblers of a lock was that he needed to attack.

J.P. launched toward Dowdy and drove his shoulder into the man's gut.

"Whoof." The wind left Dowdy like air out of a balloon.

They both hit the wet ground with a cold splash.

Dowdy pounded J.P.'s head with fists and elbows.

J.P. covered his head with both arms as rain from the ground seeped into his pants.

Dowdy scrambled to his feet.

J.P. looked up and saw the tall, bearded cameraman from KOIN news filming everything. The reporter, Amanda Kim, stood twenty feet back beneath a blue and yellow KOIN News umbrella.

"You see this?" Dowdy snatched his umbrella. "He's mad because I disclosed that Greg Newman had warned him!" Dowdy was talking to the cameraman and the reporter. "His cop dad and brother are trying to cover up the fact that he knew there was going to be a shooting and did *nothing* about it!"

J.P.'s hands got soaked as he pushed himself up to a sitting position. Then the water seeped into his knees as he worked his way back to his feet.

His head spun. He leaned over. His head hurt.

The cameraman came closer, zeroing in on his face.

J.P. saw red. He felt his head, it was soaked. He looked at his hand and it was covered in blood.

"He's stalking my girlfriend," J.P. said weakly, staggering toward Amanda Kim, but also thinking he should probably keep his mouth shut.

"J.P. Oh my gosh!" Tammy yelled and came running, splashing through the wet grass.

Laurice, the big man, her colleague, sauntered out behind Tammy.

"What'd you do to him?" Tammy screamed and put her arms around J.P. and got him to stand up straight. She gripped his shoulders and examined his head. "Come on. We need to get you inside. Come on."

Tammy glared at Dowdy and the news crew, then guided J.P. toward the front of the office as Laurice moved in to make sure Dowdy did not try to follow.

As J.P. gave up and began to walk with Tammy, he heard Dowdy telling Amanda Kim that J.P. was unstable. "And his father, the big veteran investigator, is covering up for him. Wayne Deetz is the one who needs to be investigated."

J.P. broke away from Tammy and staggered back toward them.

Tammy screamed for him to stop.

"Why don't you tell her about your affair with Greg Newman's wife!" J.P. yelled, knowing he shouldn't have said it. His anger was fueling him like a raging fire. He'd lost control and didn't care. "And about how you fought with him at Eastbank Esplanade and threw his phone in the river. Why'd you do that? Tell her about your gambling debts and money laundering—"

"Shut up!" Tammy corralled J.P. "Your dad's gonna kill you," she whispered, angrily. "Come with me."

This time, he felt Laurice's firm grip on both his arms. Without another word they spun J.P. around and led him back toward the office entrance.

He felt like he was about to pass out.

As they went, J.P. could hear Amanda Kim ask Dowdy about the affair with Jessica Newman.

Tammy was right. J.P.'s dad was going to kill him.

**30**

———————

"So, we're not going to have the weekend off, are we?" Brandon asked his dad as they ate grilled cheese sandwiches across from each other at a small table in the drafty window at Kevin's Korner Kitchen.

"You may be able to take a day, or a half-day," Deetz said. "But we've got to get this investigation wrapped up. I'm feeling the pressure from Tidwell."

"So, what's next?"

"I think I want to bring the Dowdys in together but interview them separately, one after the other," Deetz said. "That way they won't have a chance to corroborate stories."

"When?"

Deetz's phone buzzed. He glanced at it and said to Brandon, "As soon as they can get to headquarters together."

He answered the call. "J.P., what's going on? How's Tammy?"

Knowing the restaurant was empty, Deetz flicked the call to speaker so Brandon could hear.

"Everything's okay, but Tammy and I are just leaving the ER."

Deetz sat up straight and Brandon snapped to attention as well. "What happened?" Deetz said.

J.P. explained that Christopher Dowdy showed up at Tammy's office, J.P. confronted him, and they got into a scuffle.

"The bandages on my head got messed up, it was bleeding

pretty badly, so Tammy took me to ER just to be safe. They cleaned it up and re-bandaged it. I'm fine."

"Why was Dowdy there?" Brandon blurted. "What's his deal?"

"Here's the thing, the media showed up."

Deetz dropped his head.

"I think Dowdy called them and lured me into a fight—to get it on camera."

Deetz held his breath. "Did they—get it on camera?"

"Unfortunately, yeah, Dad. I'm sorry—"

"J.P.!"

"There's more. Better let me finish."

Deetz shook his head in disgust, his blood pressure skyrocketing. Brandon sat there wide-eyed.

"What?" Deetz said, exasperatedly.

When J.P. explained that he mentioned Chris Dowdy's affair with Greg Newman's wife, Deetz exploded.

"That's private! Tell me they didn't get that on camera . . ."

"They did."

Deetz stood, frustrated, leaving the phone on the table in front of Brandon. Tidwell was going to have heart failure when he heard all this.

J.P. told them he also mentioned Dowdy's fight with Greg Newman at Eastbank Esplanade when Dowdy threw Newman's phone into the river. "I may've also said something about gambling debts and money laundering," J.P. said.

"What the heck, man?" Brandon said. "This was all caught on camera? You know we're in the middle of the investigation!"

Deetz paced and didn't say a word because he knew whatever he said he would regret later.

"He played me," J.P. said in anguish. "He got me riled by following Tammy around. He wanted me to lose my temper on camera. Then all that stuff came out."

"What am I supposed to tell Tidwell?" Deetz leaned over the table and yelled into the phone. "Now the Dowdys know our hand. And for you to make it public about the affair with Jessica Newman —think how that's going to impact her!"

J.P. started to say something, but Deetz cut him off.

"You've basically made our whole investigation public. Good job, J.P. That's going to play real well at headquarters."

"Dad, I'm sorry. I screwed up. I feel terrible."

After a lengthy, awkward silence—during which Deetz determined he would explain everything to Tidwell before he saw it on the news—J.P. told them what purchasing manager Jerome Danson had said about Alexander Dowdy instructing Greg Newman to stop payment to the Indonesian bean supplier.

"He said they had some kind of deal going down," J.P. said. "I can find out more from him—"

"No. We'll talk to him." Deetz asked for Jerome's contact info.

"He wanted to keep it private," J.P. said. "I don't think he's going to talk to you."

Deetz reluctantly agreed to let J.P. follow up with Jerome.

"Where's Tammy now," Brandon said. "Are you keeping an eye on her?"

"She's taking the rest of the day off," J.P. said. "We're headed to my place."

Deetz's phone vibrated on the table.

He and Brandon both looked at the screen.

It was an incoming call from Jessica Newman.

"Uh-oh," Brandon said. "The story may've broken already. Jessica Newman's calling. We gotta take this, J.P."

Deetz and Brandon eyed each other across the table. Deetz took a deep breath and exhaled, then signaled for Brandon to accept the call and keep it on speaker.

"Hello, Mrs. Newman, this is Wayne Deetz."

"Yes, investigator. Thanks for taking my call. I have something to say to you."

"Ma'am, I'm terribly sorry. You must've seen the news . . ."

"News? No, I haven't been watching any of that. Can't handle it."

"Oh. Okay. Good." Deetz raised his eyebrows at Brandon and debated on telling her but thought better of it. "That's probably wise of you."

*Maybe she'll never even see it.*

"I'm calling because I found something . . . something you need to see."

"Oh? Okay. Brandon and I can come right over. Can you tell me anymore?"

"Just that . . ." She began to cry. "I just need to show you. I found it yesterday. I didn't sleep a wink last night. I . . . I can't keep it."

**31**

Brandon and Deetz were sitting in the Interceptor parked in Jessica Newman's driveway in Vermont Hills. Brandon felt bad for his dad, who was on the phone explaining to Sergeant Dolby Tidwell that J.P. had made some major blunders with Christopher Dowdy in front of the KOIN News crew at Tammy's office.

Even though it was only early afternoon the sky was dark and the rain continued to fall.

Brandon wondered what Jessica Newman had found. Another of her husband's guns? Drugs? A journal in which he wrote about his disturbing intentions?

"We'll be interviewing both Dowdys, back-to-back, as soon as we can," Deetz told Tidwell. "I know, sir. Yes. We want to get it over with as much as you do . . . What's that? We still think Newman acted alone, but we believe the Dowdys threatened him to get him to pay Chris Dowdy's gambling debts, we just need more proof."

Deetz glanced at Brandon and held up a finger, noting that he was almost finished.

"Is who going to press charges?" Deetz said. "Oh, you mean Jackie Brooks. Not sure about that. The problem is lack of witnesses. It's her word against his. And she seemed reluctant about going public."

Brandon could hear Tidwell raise his voice over the phone and he rambled on for a good thirty seconds.

Deetz dropped his head, closed his eyes, and ran a hand over his balding scalp.

"Okay, well, I just assumed you would want us to keep going, pursue all avenues. Fine . . . understood."

Deetz clicked his phone off and looked at Brandon. "He wants us to wrap up the case."

"What? Why?"

"He's very unhappy about all the negative press. He realizes the Dowdys may be dirty, but as long as they didn't have anything to do with the shooting—he's to the point where he doesn't care. He thinks it's more important to put the shooting to bed than to drag it out for some minor charges against the Dowdys."

"That's just frustrating!"

"He gets pressure from other places, like the mayor. It gets political."

"That really stinks."

"He said it's turning into a media circus. The mayor doesn't need any more bad PR. Neither does he. He was pretty ticked."

"But Dad, we know these guys are dirty."

Deetz nodded and opened his door. "I know, but like Tidwell just said, we don't have anything substantial. We may just have to trust God to deal with the Dowdys."

Brandon opened his door and they both got out and hurried through the rain to Jessica Newman's front door.


"GOOD TIMING," Jessica Newman said as she ushered the officers into the foyer. "I just got Daniel down for his afternoon nap. Nasty out there." She sounded out of breath, as if she was nervous.

Brandon and Deetz began walking into the room where they'd talked before, but Jessica held a hand up. "Before we sit, I'd like you to see what I found, just the way I found it," she said. "I didn't want to mess up any evidence or anything. So, if you don't mind, follow me."

It may have been Brandon's imagination, but he thought Jessica Newman had lost at least ten pounds since he'd seen her days earlier. She wore black corduroy pants, a dark green sweater, and brown loafers. Her frizzy blond hair was pulled back with a thick green headband. Her eyes looked tired and sunken.

She led them up a carpeted staircase with crooked framed family photos along the way, several including a smiling Gregory Newman, playing with his children in better days.

"Excuse the mess." She walked them into what appeared to be the master bedroom. It was small and cramped with a queen-sized bed, two oak dressers, and an out-of-date gold ceiling fan that gave off a dim, depressing light. Piles of laundry were scattered on the floor and Brandon caught a whiff of cat litter.

She opened the door to a small walk-in closet, flicked on the light, and entered. "Come in." On the right side, groups of clothes on hangers had been parted to reveal a small door down low. "This is our crawl space." She bent over and opened the door with a squeak, got down on her knees, reached in, and turned on a switch which lit a single bright bulb inside the crawl space.

"If you get down here, you'll see a duffle bag, just inside to the left." She stood with a grunt and waved a hand toward the opening.

Deetz got down on one knee and leaned into the makeshift closet. Brandon leaned over and looked in too. Deetz eyed the brown denim bag on the floor, then scanned the closet.

"I've never seen the bag before," Jessica said, standing there with her arms crossed, shivering.

On both knees, Deetz heaved the heavy bag out of the crawl space and set it on the floor.

Brandon got down on one knee.

They looked at each other and Deetz unzipped the bag and opened it wide. On top was a folded white piece of paper, which he removed and glanced at. It was a hand-written note from Gregory Newman to Jessica.

Inside the bag were stacks and stacks and stacks of hundred-dollar bills.

"Holy—" Brandon stopped when his dad glared at him.

Brandon had never seen so much money in one place.

Deetz examined the contents of the bag thoroughly and found only money, nothing else.

Then he unfolded the note and held it out so he and Brandon could read it at the same time:

*Jess,*

*There's $150,000 in this bag. Please use it for whatever you need it for.*

*If I know you, you won't want to use it. In that case, please just put it away for now. Keep it hidden in the crawl space. The years will pass and you will need it for the kids' education, weddings, birthdays, etc. Trust me. It will come in handy.*

*If you turn the money in it will probably lead to more bad press and rumors about me—and others. Please, don't stir that up. I'm begging you to simply keep it in a safe place and forget about it until you're ready to use it.*

*This is one last gesture that gives me some relief. Thank you for doing this for me.*

*Love,*
*Gregory*

Brandon and Deetz both looked up at Jessica, who shrugged and fought back a swell of emotion with a fist to her mouth.

They got to their feet.

"Do you have any idea where this may've come from?" Deetz said quietly. "Do you know if he sold off any stocks or investments recently?"

She shook her head. "That's the first thing I checked. I mean, we don't have much, but nothing's been touched. I have no idea where this could've come from."

Brandon was glad they had a new lead, but he wished Jessica could keep the money for her family.

Deetz stared down at the bag, seemingly deciding how to proceed.

The gray cat with yellow eyes appeared out of nowhere, rubbed against the bag, then began to go into the crawl space.

"No. Psst." Jessica reached down and picked up the cat, but it jumped out of her arms and ran away.

"What happens now?" Jessica said.

Brandon eyed Deetz who said, "We'll take it to headquarters and check it in as evidence."

Jessica nodded and her face contorted in a mixture of sorrow and grief.

**32**

———

"What are you thinking?" Brandon asked Deetz as he drove them back toward the city.

"I'm wondering if he somehow stole the money from Jumpy Jim's," Deetz said. "But that'd be pretty hard to do. This thing's getting weirder by the minute." Deetz had a nagging suspicion about the money, but it was too depraved to even fathom.

Brandon's phone buzzed. He glanced at it. "J.P.," he said and put him on speaker.

"Is Dad there?" J.P. said, anxiously.

"Roger that," Deetz said.

"I just hung up with Jerome Danson," J.P. said. "He overheard Alexander Dowdy tell Greg Newman that Jackie Brooks and Carrie Sandowski would be at the office Monday morning at seven—the day of the shooting."

Brandon glanced at Deetz, who was deep in thought, and whose mind was meandering further down a very dark passageway.

"Did you hear me?" J.P. said.

"Yeah. What else?" Deetz said as he continued adding two and two together.

"Jerome got the impression they were working on something together, some kind of deal." J.P. explained how Jerome had gone back for his laptop one night last week and saw Alexander and Greg sipping whiskey in Christopher's office. He said Alexander had his feet up on the desk and Greg was sitting in a chair across from him clutching a glass of whiskey with his arms resting on a duffle bag in his lap.

"A duffle bag?" Brandon said. "What color?"

"I didn't ask him."

Brandon quickly filled J.P. in on the money they'd just confiscated from Jessica Newman's crawl space.

As Deetz put together the sickening puzzle pieces, he estimated that the boys were about three steps behind him. Their minds were about to be blown.

"J.P.," Deetz said, "why would Alexander Dowdy instruct Greg Newman to stop payment to that bean supplier overseas?"

"No clue. It makes no sense," J.P. said. "I've been racking my brain on all this stuff."

"Unless," Deetz said, "that's what gave Alexander the excuse to fire Greg Newman."

The car went silent except for the hum of tires on pavement.

The boys didn't get it yet because the gruesome, hideous plan was too evil to even comprehend.

Deetz gave it a few more seconds, but he couldn't wait any longer.

"They could've planned the whole thing," he said, and left it there, waiting for the lights to come on.

"Oh no, Dad. No way." J.P.'s trembling voice came over the speaker, giving Deetz chills.

"Oh my!" Brandon's right hand shot to his mouth. His eyes bulged.

"Watch the road, son," Deetz whispered.

The unthinkable bomb that had just detonated amongst them was almost too overwhelming to speak of.

The silence indicated they were still all processing it.

Finally, Brandon spoke. "You're saying Alexander *paid* Greg Newman to kill his own son . . . and those women?"

"Dad, is that what you think?" J.P. blurted.

Deetz paused and contemplated his answer. "This money we have is a game-changer," he said. "Think about it. Maybe Alexander is sick and tired of bailing Christopher out of his gambling debts and keeping the bookies off his back; we don't know how bad that's been. He's sick of all his son's goof-ups and affairs and date rapes and domestic violence. Somehow he connects with Greg Newman and figures he can clean up most of his son's mess with one disgruntled employee opening fire on a Monday morning."

Neither of the boys said anything and Deetz wondered if his suspicion was just so far-fetched it couldn't possibly be true.

"It adds up—but it's *sick*," J.P. said. "I can't imagine anyone being so cold-blooded. That's his son!"

Brandon stared straight ahead at the road with his mouth hanging open as if in a trance. Deetz wondered what he was thinking. He was usually so outspoken.

"J.P., let us hang up," Deetz said. "Not a word to anyone. We need to get this money back to headquarters and get the Dowdys in for questioning, right now."

Brandon continued to drive in silence. They were three blocks from headquarters.

"Dad, that can't be true," Brandon spoke in monotone. "I don't believe anyone can be that messed up."

"I hope you're right, son. And I would never suggest such a thing unless I thought it was a real possibility."

"Man, I guess I never fully realized the depths of darkness you've had to immerse yourself in to be good at what you do."

He was right. And Deetz was thrilled that in eight months he would no longer have to plumb those depths of darkness anymore.

"Has it ever been too much for you?" Brandon said.

Deetz nodded. "Yes. I don't know how I made it all those years when I didn't lean on God like I do now. So that's been key. But so are the relationships with good counselors like the one you're seeing."

Deetz's phone vibrated. He began working it out of his pocket.

"And that's why it's also really important that you take every vacation, day off, holiday possible. You need time away from the streets to recharge."

Deetz looked at his screen but didn't recognize the caller's number.

"Wayne Deetz," he answered.

"It's Darlene Dowdy. Chris just blew in here and he's acting crazy." She whispered frantically. "His dad's on the way and says he needs to see both of us."

"Okay, keep calm," Deetz said. "You're at your home—where we met?"

Brandon eyed Deetz.

"Yes. Can you come?" she said. "He doesn't know I'm calling."

Deetz glanced at Brandon, who'd slowed down and was poised to turn on a dime.

"We'll be there," Deetz said.

"Wait, I need to tell you, he has a gun, Chris does. Text me when you get here and I'll buzz you in the glass doors from my phone. I'll try to leave our condo door ajar but I can't promise."

Just then, Deetz heard Christopher Dowdy scream Darlene's name and the call ended.

**33**

———————

Brandon turned the Interceptor around in a flash and hit the siren while Deetz radioed for backup.

"What are we getting into?" Brandon said breathlessly.

Deetz was busy on the radio.

They weren't far from Dowdy's condo.

Deetz finished the call and addressed Brandon. "Christopher is armed. We need to assume the dad may be too. It could get hot. These guys are both loose cannons. It'll be close quarters in there. But Darlene's the one we're worried about. As far as I'm concerned, she's in danger right now and we're going to make sure everything stays cool."

"Right, right," Brandon said.

"Keep it cool. Everyone stays calm. Even if we have to just get her out of there."

Within minutes, they bumped into the parking deck at a high rate of speed and Deetz turned off the siren. As Brandon maneuvered the Interceptor up and around toward the eleventh floor with his heart racing as they got closer.

Deetz closed his eyes and said: "The fear of man brings a snare, but the one who trusts in the Lord will be protected, safe, secure, set on high."

"Amen to that," Brandon said.

~

BRANDON PARKED the Interceptor about four spaces away from the glass doors leading to the hallway of the Dowdy's condo.

"That's Christopher's SUV," he told Deetz, pointing to the gangster-looking matte black car. "I guess we don't know what Alexander drives?"

"No, could be any of these," Deetz said. "Let's throw this money in the way-back, just to be safe." Deetz grabbed the duffle and got out of the Interceptor. He met Brandon around back of the vehicle.

Deetz hit the button for the hatchback and as it arose his phone buzzed. He got it out and glanced at the screen. It was a text from Darlene Dowdy: "Alexander not here yet . . ."

Deetz's mind exploded with alarm.

As his head jerked up to scan the premises and his right hand instinctively went for his firearm, he was simultaneously overcome by a sickening feeling of dread and guilt for having assumed the elder Dowdy was already inside the condo.

"Stop right there."

It was Alexander Dowdy.

He stood in a nearby shadow pointing a compact assault rifle at both officers. "Don't move a muscle. I'm not afraid to use this." He spoke calmly and stood very still.

Deetz looked at Brandon and nodded slowly, motioning for him to do as the man instructed.

"Set the bag down."

Deetz did so.

"Both of you raise your hands up—way up."

They did. Brandon's eyes were scared, but fierce.

"It's not good that you found the bag." Alexander stepped into the light, appearing much more massive than he had come across on TV at the press conference. He wore an expensive dark gray suit and red tie with a matching red handkerchief sticking neatly out the breast pocket.

He approached them slowly.

"Did Darlene contact you?" Alexander said.

"Yes," Deetz said.

Alexander clenched his teeth and huffed. "Did you call for backup?"

Brandon looked at Deetz, who turned to Alexander and said yes.

"Hmm." Alexander stepped closer. "Dad, I need you to slowly pick up the bag and put it in the backseat of that brown Mercedes right there. Doors are open."

Deetz started to do so, thinking he would make a move for his Glock once at the car.

"Hold up," Alexander said. "First, remove your gun belt, slowly, and set it on the ground. Nice and easy. You too, young man."

Deetz locked eyes with Brandon and nodded, then slowly did as he was told. Brandon did the same.

"Good. Now step away from the belts. Dad, put the money in the Benz."

With the assault rifle trained on them, they had no recourse. They had just set down their utility belts, which included their guns, tasers, pepper spray, and ASP batons.

Once Deetz shut the back door of the Mercedes, Alexander said, "Now I need you to cancel the call for backup." He pointed his gun at Brandon. "Get over by your dad."

After more prompting from Alexander, Deetz walked to the driver's door of the Interceptor with Brandon at his side. Alexander followed closely.

"Call in," Alexander said.

Deetz got the mic from his shoulder, called headquarters, and waited for a response.

"Say it was a false alarm," Alexander instructed. "Say you're here. Everything is fine. You're leaving. I want to hear it all."

Deetz did not like the thoroughness and order demonstrated by Alexander. He racked his brain to think of some secret radio speak he could use to let the station know they were under duress, but Alexander had moved within several feet and Deetz was forced to do exactly as he'd been told.

"Good. Now toss your phones into the car."

Deetz and Brandon looked at each other, feeling the desperation heightening as each hope was stripped away.

"Hurry up."

They tossed their phones into the Interceptor.

Alexander slammed the door and waved his weapon toward the glass doors. "Go on, lead the way. We're going inside. You've been here before."

Deetz and Brandon started walking with their hands up, about five feet in front of Alexander. As they passed their utility belts, Deetz wondered what Alexander planned to do with them, if anything.

Without missing a beat, Alexander bent down, scooped a gun from one of the belts, and jammed it in the front pocket of his pants. He then tossed the belt against a wall in the shadows. "Keep going," he ordered. Then he grabbed the other gun, put it in his coat pocket, and tossed that belt in the same direction.

"Press the button. You know how it works," Alexander said. "They'll buzz us in and we'll get this party started."

**34**

———

Brandon's heart banged in his chest as he and Deetz led the way down the sleek, carpeted hallway with the amber-colored lights and mural of Portland. Someone had buzzed them in quickly. Alexander was just steps behind them with the assault rifle at their backs.

Deetz seemed calm, but Brandon detected a flash of desperation in his eyes when the guns and phones were taken.

Straight ahead on the left, the door of the Dowdy condo opened, and Christopher Dowdy leaned his head into the hallway, looking right at them. He froze when he saw the two cops being led at gunpoint by his old man.

"What the . . ." Christopher cussed and chuckled and stepped fully into the hallway, wearing his trademark white athletic shorts, black windbreaker, and Nikes. He shook his head and smiled with the shiny silver Bluetooth earbud bulging from the side of his head.

"Hurry up and get inside," Alexander said to all of them.

Darlene Dowdy's head dropped in regret when she saw the officers in custody. She backed up in the entryway with her hands clasped behind her back. She wore baggy faded denim overalls and a white, long-sleeved T-shirt, white Hokas, and a gold bracelet around one ankle.

With a nervous mixture of expletives, Christopher asked his dad what was going on. Deetz could see the heavy shape of a gun weighing down his right coat pocket.

Alexander quietly closed the door of the condo, pointed the assault rifle at the Deetzes, and instructed everyone to go into the living room.

Christopher blabbed nervously, again inquiring what was going on.

"Quiet, son. Just. Be. Quiet," Alexander said. "I need to think. Everyone go to the sunken area and sit—now please."

"Where'd you find that bad boy?" Christopher said anxiously, referring to his dad's assault rifle.

Alexander stopped, glared at Christopher, and said, "Are you aware it was your lovely bride who called these fine men in blue?"

Christopher scowled, his nostrils flared, and his head swiveled toward Darlene. He cussed and raised a backhand. She cowered and held up her arms to protect herself.

"No, son." Alexander shook his head and Christopher lowered his hand. "It's water under the bridge. The fact is, they found something they shouldn't have, something incriminating. Didn't you, boys? I said, everyone sit down. You too, son."

Darlene walked away from Christopher and threw herself into a chair, but he followed her and sat on a white leather couch adjacent to her. Deetz followed Christopher probably to be closest to the gun, but Brandon made eye contact with Deetz, gave a small nod, and sat next to Christopher on the couch. If anyone was going to wrestle him for the firearm it would be Brandon; he didn't want his dad fighting either Dowdy.

Meanwhile, Brandon scanned the room for anything he could use for a weapon. The only thing notable was a contemporary piece of clay pottery on the coffee table near him that looked like it weighed about three pounds. Otherwise, there were the bottles at the bar. That was it.

"If you let us take you in right now for questioning, Alexander, if you come peaceably, we'll forget what's happened here so far today," Deetz lied.

Alexander had not entered the sunken sitting area, so he towered over them looking very in control holding the assault rifle with the floor-to-ceiling windows behind him.

"How generous of you," Alexander said.

"What was found that was so incriminating?" Christopher said, anxiously.

Brandon and Deetz looked at Alexander to see how he would respond.

Alexander tilted his head and stared at his son with a look of disgust.

"What?" Christopher said.

"It's all about you, isn't it, son?"

"What?"

"Everything. Everything's about you. Your gambling. Your toys. Your women. Life has always revolved around Christopher Rutherford Dowdy."

Christopher chuckled nervously and began to stand up.

"Don't!" Alexander pointed the assault rifle at his son. "Stay where you are."

"Jessica Newman called us, Christopher," Deetz said. "She found a bag with one-hundred-fifty thousand dollars in it. Gregory had left it for her."

Christopher squinted at Deetz, glanced at his dad, and looked back at Deetz.

"It was blood money," Deetz said.

"Oh my gosh!" Darlene screamed. "Oh my gosh! No. No. No."

Christopher stared at her, still confused.

Alexander raised his eyebrows and looked pleased the story was finally out.

"I don't get it," Christopher said.

"Your dad paid Greg Newman to do what he did—to kill you, you idiot!" Darlene said.

"The women, too," Deetz said.

Christopher stood abruptly.

"No you don't," Alexander raised the gun at him.

Christopher stood there, mouth open, glaring at his dad. A tear streaked down his cheek. He took a step toward his dad.

"Stop!" Alexander thundered.

"Tell me the truth," Christopher said.

"It's true." Alexander stepped closer to the sunken area and Christopher. "Sit. I'll explain."

"No!" Christopher took another two steps toward his dad. They were twelve feet from each other. "Talk, now!"

Brandon looked at Deetz whose eyes went from the gun in Christopher's coat pocket to the piece of pottery on the table.

"All your selfish life I've been used by you and embarrassed by you," Alexander said. "I've covered up for you, lied for you, made excuses for you—*paid* for your mistakes! You've bled me of hundreds of thousands of dollars. You've ruined my reputation."

Christopher had morphed into a zombie and began walking slowly toward his father, seemingly not caring that he could be gunned down in an instant.

Alexander took a step back. "When you humiliated Gregory Newman in public and threw his phone into the river—after having an affair with his wife—that was the last straw. He told me all about it. He was at the end of his rope. I simply gave him a little incentive—"

Christopher charged his father, who braced his legs, locked aim with the assault rifle, and blasted three rapid-fire rounds.

The room lit up and smoke filled the air.

Darlene screamed and Deetz and Brandon stood up.

Blood splattered Christopher's coat and he dropped at the edge of the sunken living area. It looked like two of the three rounds had entered his upper body. He screamed in pain.

"SIT DOWN!" Alexander ordered the others.

Reluctantly, Deetz and Brandon lowered back to their seats. But Darlene ignored him and crawled to her husband, who had rolled onto his back with his mouth and eyes wide open.

"There you go again, only thinking of yourself," Alexander said.

Brandon realized the stakes had just elevated and he could see the sliver of concern in his dad's eyes.

Darlene grabbed a pillow from the couch and pushed it against her husband's wounds.

"This was supposed to be all wrapped up today with a nice bow," Alexander said. "Christopher, you were going to poison Darlene and then take your own life. And now all the sudden you've been shot, and we have two of Portland's finest involved. Messy, messy—"

As if on cue, Darlene Dowdy raised her husband's gun in both hands, screamed, and blasted Alexander before he realized what was happening. She fired three rounds. Two misses blew out the glass wall behind him and one exploded in Alexander's stomach.

When Brandon saw Alexander grimace and crumple to the ground, he dove at Darlene, grabbed the gun, and trained it on Alexander.

Deetz was over the big man within seconds, kicking the assault rifle away, and snatching the guns from Alexander's pockets.

As Brandon watched his dad read Alexander his rights and as he watched Christopher gasp for air while his wife shouted to the nine-one-one operator on her phone—every sound in the room seemed to vacuum up and away.

Silence rang in Brandon's ears.

His temples pounded.

His vision bleached.

He collapsed to the floor, still holding the gun weakly.

"Brandon. What is it? You okay?"

Brandon nodded, trying to act strong for his dad.

"Find something more to stop his bleeding." Deetz nodded at Christopher.

*Why do you care?* Brandon thought.

*Let him die. Let them both die.*

"Hey, buddy—we've got a job to do," Deetz said. "Are you good?"

Brandon looked at Christopher. Then at Alexander. Then at Deetz, who was kneeling over Alexander, pressing down as hard as he could with his bare hands on the man's bleeding wound.

Looking at the Dowdys, then at his dad, was like looking from utter ruin and darkness and evil—to brilliant light and truth and goodness.

What an amazing father Brandon had been given in Deetz. A remarkable cop, husband, dad, and role model. A godly man.

A keen and overwhelming sense of gratitude flooded Brandon.

And he realized, he could be like his dad, he could follow in his footsteps—salt and light in an evil world.

"I'm good," Brandon finally answered, wiping the sweat from his forehead.

On his knees, he ripped a small throw blanket from a nearby chair and headed toward Christopher Dowdy.

# EPILOGUE

It was late Friday night two weeks after the shootout at the Dowdy condo. Deetz was the only one still awake at the house, where he sat quietly in his favorite chair in the dimly lit family room, swiping through pictures on his phone taken earlier that evening at Brandon's college graduation ceremony.

He stopped and smiled at the picture of Brandon, wearing his black gown, with an arm around his mom on one side and sister Leena on the other, and flanked by J.P. and Tammy. Everyone in the shot was laughing because Leena had just held up Brandon's graduation cap, which she'd taken the liberty to decorate with the words "Po-Po" in masking tape.

Deetz flicked the phone off, leaned back in the chair, kicked his shoes off, and put his feet up on the coffee table. He was about ready to turn in for the night. He heard the heat kick on. It would be dropping into the high thirties overnight. He was looking forward to having Saturday and Sunday off and he knew Brandon was too.

Both Dowdys had survived the gunshot wounds they'd sustained two weeks earlier and were in separate hospitals in the city. Christopher was worse than his father and was still in serious condition, while Alexander had started daily rehab and was expected to be released within a week. Upon their release, both men would be arraigned on multiple felony charges.

Detailed police findings from their numerous computers, cell phones, and company records had proven that Laser Direct was indeed a shadow company—with only four hourly employees—set up by Alexander Dowdy for the sole purpose of extorting and laundering funds from Jumpy Jim's. What Alexander and Christopher did with the funds they syphoned was still being determined, but at least $144,000 of it had been used to pay local bookies for Christopher's out-of-control gambling debts.

Burner phones were used by the Dowdys for many of their unethical undertakings, including repeated threats made toward Gregory Newman, supposedly from an organized crime group, but proven to be from Christopher Dowdy.

Once Jackie Brooks heard about all the charges coming down against the Dowdys, she threw her hat in the ring and retained one of the city's finest prosecuting attorneys to press charges against Christopher for rape. Carrie Sandowski's family and fiancé followed suit by hiring that same attorney to bring coercion, sexual harassment, and other charges against Christopher Dowdy.

Deetz closed his eyes and recalled with lament how floored Brandon and J.P. had been when they'd learned the gruesome details about Alexander's plans to murder Christopher and Darlene Dowdy.

The old man had gone there that day with plans to kill them both and make it look like a murder-suicide. In Alexander's suit coat pocket authorities found two rare and expensive potassium cyanide capsules, which would have killed Christopher and Darlene within seconds. Also in Alexander's possession was a thumb drive containing a suicide note he'd written but signed in Christopher's name. The elder Dowdy planned to plant it on Christopher's computer and print out a copy to leave near the bodies. Of course, the note blamed everything on Christopher and left Alexander smelling like a rose. Alexander was being charged with two counts of first-degree attempted murder, solicitation of murder for hire, and an assortment of additional felony charges.

Deetz chuckled to himself because Brandon said he'd been to see Dr. Wallender twice since the shootings at the Dowdy condo. He'd joked that the events had given him a good excuse to go see the woman, who was apparently a knockout. But Deetz knew

Brandon better than that—he wouldn't waste his time or hers if she wasn't helping him work through the trauma of the past three weeks.

Deetz leaned over, picked up his shoes and phone with a sigh, got up, and walked into the dark kitchen. He set the things on the island, opened the fridge, looked around, saw nothing appealing, and closed it, ready for bed.

His phone buzzed and glowed on the island.

He went over and glanced at it.

A text from Brandon: "Thanks for coming to graduation tonight, Dad."

Deetz smiled and texted back: "We're extremely proud of you, son. Congrats!"

Brandon: "You're up late."

Deetz: "About to turn in. Where are you? Out celebrating?"

Brandon: "Out with a small group from the church I went to Sunday."

Deetz: "Cool. What are you doing?"

Brandon: "Bowling. It's actually a really good group of people."

Deetz: "Fantastic."

Brandon: "Night Pops. Tell Mom I love her."

Deetz: "Ok. Be safe. I love you."

The phone went black.

The kitchen was dark.

Deetz stood there for a moment. He thanked God Brandon may've found a church and a new group of friends.

It was now late May. Deetz had seven months remaining on the force until he would hang it up for good at the end of the year. Until then, he planned to continue pouring as much police knowledge into Brandon as he could with the time they had left together in the field.

Deetz was actually getting excited about not being a cop anymore. In many ways it would be a great relief.

He got his shoes and headed for the steps.

*Who knows, maybe Tidwell will ask me to be the police chaplain someday?*

# WHAT'S NEXT FROM CRESTON?

If you're ready to continue the remarkable story of Wayne Deetz and his beloved family, check out book six in the Signs of Life Series on **Amazon:**

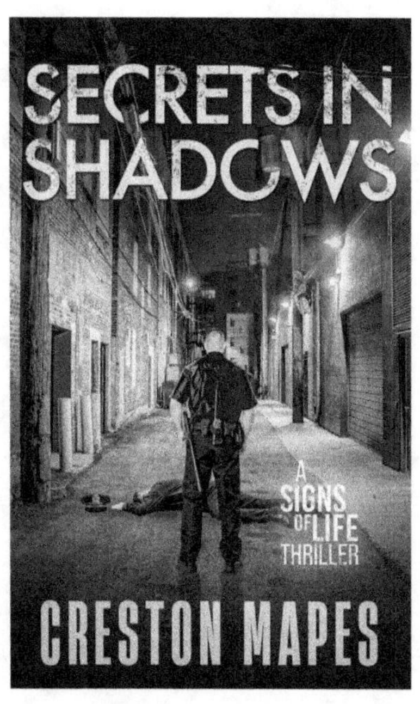

# ABOUT THE AUTHOR

**Creston Mapes** grew up in northeast Ohio, where he has fond memories of living with his family of five in the upstairs portion of his dad's early American furniture store - The Weathervane Shop. Creston was not a good student, but the one natural talent he possessed was writing.

He set type by hand and cranked out his own neighborhood newspaper as a kid, then went on to graduate with a degree in journalism from Bowling Green State University. Creston was a newspaper reporter and photographer in Ohio and Florida, then moved to Atlanta, Georgia, for a job as a creative copywriter.

Creston served for a stint as a creative director, but quickly learned he was not cut out for management. He went out on his own as a freelance writer in 1991 and, over the next 30 years, did work for Chick-fil-A, Coca-Cola, The Weather Channel, Oracle, ABC-TV, TNT Sports, colleges and universities, ad agencies, and more. He's ghost-written more than ten non-fiction books.

Along the way, Creston has written 13 contemporary thrillers, achieved Amazon Bestseller status multiple times, and had one of his novels (*Nobody*) optioned as a major motion picture.

Creston married his fourth-grade sweetheart, Patty, and they have four amazing adult children. Creston loves his part-time job as an usher at local venues where he gets to see all the latest-greatest concerts and sporting events. He enjoys reading, fishing, thrifting, bocci, painting, pickleball, time with his family, and dates with his wife.

Keep informed of special deals, giveaways, new releases, and exclusive updates from Creston: **CrestonMapes.com/contact**

For Creston's eBooks, audiobooks, and paperbacks: **Amazon.-com/author/crestonmapes**

### STAND ALONE THRILLERS
*I Am In Here*
*Nobody*

### SIGNS OF LIFE SERIES
*Signs of Life*
*Let My Daughter Go*
*I Pick You*
*Charm Artist*
*Son & Shield*
*Secrets in Shadows*

### THE CRITTENDON FILES
*Fear Has a Name*
*Poison Town*
*Sky Zone*

### ROCK STAR CHRONICLES
*Dark Star: Confessions of a Rock Idol*
*Full Tilt*